That Girl on ௴௴

A Novel
by
Maharana G

Cover by:
Sudhir Shetty

This book is a work of fiction. Though the characters are mostly relatable, any resemblance to actual persons, living or dead, or actual events is purely coincidental.

The purpose of this book is to bring an interesting story to you, entertain you, and communicate with you.

Copyright © 2023 Maharana Ganesh
All rights reserved.

No part of this book may be reproduced or stored in a retrieval system or transmitted in any form or by any means, electronic, mechanical, photocopying, recording, or otherwise, without written permission of the author.

To all of YOU, my readers

Characters

Padma/Devi – The protagonist
Venkat – Padma's boyfriend
Subbu – Venkat's elder brother
Laxman – Padma's elder brother
Appa Rao – Venkat's father
Aman a.k.a Mummy – The artist
Akash – Aman's best friend
Ayush – Aman's friend
Ghalib – Aman's friend
Suman Kirad – Aman's mother
Arvinder Kirad a.k.a Mogambo – Aman's father
K Srinivas – Padma's father
Geeta – Padma's mother
Shanti – Laxman's wife, Padma's sister-in-law
Lucy – The kitten

Chapter 1: The Retract

Wherever one can see, there are mountains, mountains, and mountains in this part of the world. The serene greenery of the region fills human beings with utmost peace and positivity. What else should one expect on vacation? Well, our thoughts are triggered by our mental state. The surroundings can make an impact, but the state of our inner world overpowers it. Padma has lost her peace of mind. Hence, this extraordinary beauty of nature is of no value to her at the moment.

"No, I don't have an option. I will have to end it here; I have to die. How will I be able to show this face to my people?" She keeps murmuring, standing at the edge of a hilltop. The depth of the valley is visible to her. She has come here to commit suicide but is scared of heights; she has always been acrophobic.

The girl in her early 20s must have gone in a loop for the last two hours or so—moving one step ahead and then retracting from the act. Her legs are shivering as she is extremely nervous and is not quite sure if this is her last resort.

1

Even though Padma is in distress now, she wishes she could live. Live to get married. Live to have children. Live to see her children get married. And live to see the children of her children. Alas, that doesn't seem to be happening. Finally, she sits down on a rock nearby and tries to revisit her memory lane. She wants to judge herself once again. Isn't there any way she can go back to her normal life? She wants to find one reason, just one reason to live. She decides to give it another try to analyze her situation.

Padma is from Srikakulam, a small town in Andhra Pradesh, the southern part of India. She used to go to the city college. It was normal practice for students in the college to bunk classes. However, Padma wouldn't do that—not because she was a brilliant student but because she had a liking for Venkat, her classmate and childhood friend.

Unlike Padma, Venkat was studious. He would always sit in the front row. He would always answer the teachers' questions first. Padma would never dare sit next to Venkat. What if the teacher asked her a question? If she didn't give the correct answer, everyone would laugh at her. Particularly, Venkat would consider her dumb. No, she wouldn't do that. The back bench was safe for two reasons—avoiding the questions and safely staring at Venkat.

The studious Venkat didn't dislike the backbenchers though. He used to hang out with them every day, have lunch with them, and play carrom in the common room. Out of all the backbenchers, he liked Padma the most. He was in love with her. Recently, their love for each other was out in the open. In college, the rule was that if a couple announced their relationship, nobody would ask any of them out.

Venkat was good at chemistry, and Padma was happy to have good chemistry with him. Everything was going well between them. They had already decided to inform their parents about their relationship and express their desire to marry each other after they passed out of college this year.

As expected, Venkat passed the Bachclor of Science final examination with flying colors, and Padma somehow managed to pass.

"I have scored better in the exam, but you will score well in the exam of our life," Venkat told Padma to cheer her up after checking her results.

Padma comes back to the present. "But you have failed me, Venky?" she says and heads to the cliff. In a minute, she comes back to the rock and sits on it again.

Padma picks a stick lying nearby and hits the rock with it, applying all her strength as she continues recalling the occurrences in chronological order.

It's time for both of them to talk to their parents about their marriage. Twenty-two didn't seem too soon for them to get married. There were couples in the immediate society who got married even earlier. They didn't even anticipate any objection from their parents as they belonged to the same community. All that they needed to do was to inform their parents. That's it.

Studying was a formality. Neither Venkat nor Padma intended to use that knowledge and certificate to pursue a career. They would join their parents' business. Venkat's family had a spices business, and Padma's family was into that of tea leaves.

In their meeting at a friend's wedding, they decided to talk to their parents about their marriage the next morning. Everything was set. Venkat got up in the morning. Everyone in the family had already got up. His elder brother had gone to oversee the work in their paddy fields. His father was cleaning his teeth with a stem of neem.

Venkat was seeing his father's actions. As soon as the latter is done with the bath, Venkat thought it was the right time to talk to him. He was about to carry out his mission when his brother came home running. He was bleeding in the head.

"Subbu…" his father called out and ran to his brother. "What happened, Subbu? Did you have an accident?"

After sitting on the verandah and drinking a glass of water, Subbu described the incident.

Laxman and Subbu fought over the water supply to their fields. They attacked each other with iron tools used for cultivation. Both got injured in the fight.

"Venky, go inside and bring the first aid box," his father instructed.

As Venkat ran inside, his heart was pounding. He would never be able to reveal his relationship with Padma to his father. He was in deep trouble. His life had turned upside down within a minute.

Appa Rao's family was known for keeping their enmity with people. If they fought with anyone once, they would not patch up for a lifetime. Appa Rao had never talked to his sister after a minor argument. Unfortunately, Venkat was his youngest son. Then onwards, the family would keep the rivalry with Laxman's family, which included Padma.

Subbu and Laxman were banned from going to the fields by their respective parents then onwards to avoid any further violence. Hence, Venkat and Padma took charge. In the morning, they would go to the fields to oversee work. Five more days of work were remaining. Afterward, the crops were to be left alone for a couple of months.

For two days, Venkat and Padma avoided each other. Third day onwards, they made the arrangements for a discussion. A few yards away from each other, they stood on the ridge between their fields, both looking at their respective fields.

"What do you think, Venky? Is it possible for us to marry?" Padma asked.

"I don't know. I don't think my parents will agree to our proposal," Venkat replied in a low voice sadly. It was hardly audible to her, but she got the message from his expression.

"What do you think then? Should we forget each other?" Padma asked.

Venkat didn't know what to say. He remained silent.

"What do you think? Tell me," Padma asked again.

"I think that's our destiny," he struggled with his voice but managed to say.

Padma could see he was in tears.

"If that was our destiny, why did you agree to this plan?" Padma says as she comes back to the present. She approaches the cliff again and comes back to the rock.

The next day they met on the ridge and took their positions to talk. Padma had news for Venkat that day.

"Some people are coming home for my marriage proposal," she broke the news.

Venkat was shocked. "Isn't it too early for you? You are only 22," he inquired.

"If our brothers hadn't fought, we would have got married next month. And my father would have gifted us this piece of land over which our brothers fought," Padma pointed at the piece of land in front of her.

They had a long discussion that day. It could have been one of their last meetings.

The last thing that Padma said before they left the field was, "In school, college, everywhere, you were a frontbencher. I always took a seat behind you from where I could see you. You never looked back. Here as well, you are not looking back. I am the only one looking at you with hope. I should have known about your cowardliness before getting involved with you."

The next day when they met, they were perhaps meeting for the last time. That day was the last day of work on the fields for the season.

"I was thinking about you the whole night," Venkat started the conversation that time. But his words fell on deaf ears.

"The boy and their family have given their nod for me," Padma said.

"I couldn't sleep the entire night," Venkat too continued without listening to her.

"Next week is the ENGAGEMENT, Venky," Padma tried to make sure Venkat listened to her.

"You were not right about me yesterday," Venkat said. He had decided to ignore what Padma was saying at the moment. It didn't matter to him at all.

"As far as studies are concerned, I did well. I focused on it. That doesn't mean I had no interest in you. Life is not all about love. It's a mixture of a lot of things. When I studied, I studied well. And, when I was in a relationship, I maintained it well," he added.

"Why are you saying all this now? It's all over," Padma questioned the timing of the argument.

"Because I don't think we are done with it, Padma. Our brothers fought over a silly matter. Why should we sacrifice our love for that?" Venkat was a little loud. He realized that and decided to be careful thereafter.

This was what Padma wanted to hear from the boy. Thereafter, the conversation went the normal way.

"But... isn't it too late? How will we convince our parents?" She expressed her fears.

"We will never be able to convince them. We will have to elope," he said confidently.

"It was you who proposed the idea. Then, why did you backtrack?" Padma says to herself as she wipes her tears and then gets up. For a change, she doesn't walk to the cliff but takes a look at the mountain range all around and comes back to the rock.

"What are you saying? Don't you want to try even once?" asked a shocked Padma.

"No, Padma. You see, now you are able to come to the fields and we are talking here. That's only because they don't know about our relationship. Once they come to know about us, they will lock us up in a room," Venkat tried to sensitize her with the hypothesis.

"Then?"

"Let's elope before your engagement," he said confidently.

"Why not now?"

"We will need some money. I will try to get some tonight and you also try. We don't know how life is going to be henceforth," he said.

"If possible, will we elope tonight?" Padma checked.

"Yes, we will have to," Venkat replied.

They knew the stories of a couple of friends who had eloped and then came back and got married as their parents accepted their relationship later. Maybe those success stories gave them the courage to take the bold step.

They executed the plan well. Venkat stole money from his father's treasure box, and Padma stole jewelry from her mother's treasure box. Early in the morning, when everyone was deep asleep, they left for Srikakulam railway station. They knew, if their people got up and didn't find them, the first place they would search was the railway station. Hence, they boarded the very first train that arrived at the station. It was Shalimar express. It reached Hyderabad late in the evening.

Of course, much before going to Hyderabad, they got calls from their family members. They had to switch off their phones to avoid communication. However, Hyderabad was not safe either. They have many relatives in Hyderabad. Some must already be waiting at the station to trace them.

So, they hopped onto another train. It was Dakshin express, going to Delhi. They got to know about it after a few stations. As it was off-season, there were many vacant seats. The couple traveled without tickets, and nobody caught them. They got lucky somehow. Once they saw a ticket checker, they went into the toilet and locked themselves up in one toilet for 15 minutes.

It was crazy and adventurous for both. Either love or survival has the power to make people do such craziness.

After a 30-hour journey, they reached Delhi. Initially, they worked at a stall of a fast-food chain. But thereafter, both got jobs at a call center. Within three months in Delhi, it seemed they were all settled.

However, they couldn't free their minds from the thoughts of what might be happening at home all that while. They couldn't get in touch with anyone they knew of.

After a few days, they came across one person from Srikakulam in Delhi. Venkat knew him and addressed him as 'anna'. Neither Venkat nor Padma did see any risk there.

However, Venkat started behaving mysteriously afterward and kept meeting that person. He didn't reveal any details of their meeting to Padma. She suspected something fishy but didn't bother much to check with him.

The love birds finally planned to come to Shimla on a vacation for a week. It was a Saturday. They took a train to Kalka, and from there, they switched the train to reach Shimla. Throughout the travel, Venkat seemed lost. He continued his mysterious behavior even after they reached Shimla. Something was eating him up from within, which he couldn't reveal to Padma.

Monday morning, when Padma got up in the hotel, Venkat was nowhere in the vicinity. She looked everywhere for him madly, but with no results; she called him numerous times but got no response.

"Oh, my God! I hope he is fine. Is it some kind of prank?" Padma kept thinking while looking for Venkat. It was only in the evening that she got a message from him. By that time, she had exhausted all her options and felt crazy and tired. Receiving a

message from Venkat was a relief. The day until then passed like a year for her. She quickly opened the message.

"Amma fell sick because of us. I am going to Srikakulam to meet her," the message read.

Padma called Venkat as soon as she read the message. His phone was switched off. She sent message after message. No response to any of them.

After spending two days without Venkat in the hotel room, mostly sobbing, she got a message on her phone. She was not expecting any message from Venkat. Still, she checked her phone. It hit the last nail in the coffin.

"I won't be able to come back to you. My mother fell sick after we eloped. Your parents have filed a police case against me. You also come back to Srikakulam," read the message.

"How can I go back home? You are a boy. Everyone will accept you. Boys in society are like pots made of brass. The more you rub it, the more they shine. But we girls… we are earthen pots. We never get back to our primary form. My family is not waiting to give me a warm welcome. Instead, they must be waiting to kill me. I can never get my normal life back. If this was supposed to happen, why did you take that bold step earlier?" Padma screams and heads to the cliff. This time, she is determined to jump off and put an end to everything.

"O, God! Please forgive me. I am coming back to you. I have nobody who loves me. Everyone I know must be hating me now," when Padma is about to jump, she hears someone speaking hysterically.

"Who is this? There was nobody here till now," she wonders and looks around.

Her eyes fall to the other corner of the cliff as it looks like a boy is standing there. There are rocks and some bushes between them. They are so close to each other that not only she can see him, but their voices can also reach each other.

"Hello!" Padma screams in an attempt to talk to the boy. He is all alone. She guesses the boy must have come here to commit suicide.

The boy looks at Padma. He gets anxious and looks terrified.

"No, no, please don't jump. Talk to me. I may be able to help you," Padma says as she fears he will jump off after hearing her voice.

"How can you help me? You don't even know me! My own people have disowned me. What can I expect from a stranger, that too, from a girl?" The boy says in an uninterested tone.

"Trust me, life is not only about the people who you have known so far. It is much beyond that. You can meet new people; you can build new relationships; and you can live for a hundred years happily with them, loving them and being loved," Padma tries to persuade him.

"It's easy to give a speech. Only those who have been hurt know the pain," the boy says as he moves a step closer to the cliff.

"Please stop. I can prove my point," Padma almost starts crying.

"It's not that I have never been hurt. I know the pain. My boyfriend with whom I eloped has left me alone here and gone back to his family. Now, I cannot go back to my family. But, for that reason, I am not going to commit suicide. I am going to start a new life. It's cowardice to end one's own life," she cites her example to convince the boy. She feels a personal connection may help in convincing. And she is not wrong. It looks like her argument and example are working on the boy who is now willing to pursue the conversation.

"Oh, so you are all alone now. Didn't you feel hurt?" he asks while wiping his tears.

"I did. But I am not going to end my life for that," Padma speaks at the top of her voice, following which she starts coughing. She has already got a sore throat as a side effect of sobbing continuously for two days.

"Wait, I got water," says the boy and runs to her with the water bottle he is carrying in his bag. He opens the bottle himself and hands it over to her.

"Were you going to jump off along with the bag?" she asks before starting to drink some water.

"I didn't realize that," he replies while catching his breath.

They sit on the rock together for some time, looking at the horizon as the sun sets.

"What were you doing here alone?" the boy asks now that it looks like the disastrous plans have been dropped.

"I wanted to see the setting sun from here to compare it to my life. And when I did that, I realized…" she pauses to think.

"You realized?" the boy is restless to learn about the complete thought.

"And, then I realized the sun would rise again. There would be light in my life again," she sounds like a philosopher. "And then..." she pauses again.

"And then?" he wants to get more thoughts from her.

Padma looks at the boy curiously. He is asking questions like a good student.

"And, then I met a stupid boy who was going to commit suicide for some stupid girl," she jokes.

"How did you know it was about a girl?" the boy exclaims.

"It was obvious. What else could it be at this age!" Padma says as she gets up.

They walk together back to the main road and then to the hotel in which Padma is staying.

"Now that you have nowhere to go, why don't you come back to Delhi with us?" the boy checks.

"Meaning you have someone with you," Padma checks.

"Yes. We are a group of friends. We are driving back to Delhi tomorrow morning," he says.

Padma thinks about the plan. She doesn't want to stay in Shimla anymore. But going with a stranger doesn't seem to be a good idea either.

"I don't even know your name," she says quite hesitantly.

"My name is Aman. I am from Delhi. Now, you know me. Come on. You saved my life. Let me drop you at your destination. It will make me feel better," Aman tries to convince her.

Padma has to agree. As it is, she is going back to Delhi. It's better to travel with this group. They share their phone numbers and then bid goodbye for the evening.

Chapter 2: The Artistic Trip

"Mummy!" called out one of Aman's friends. He hadn't got ready till then. The boys' group was supposed to leave for Shimla in the morning.

"Aunty, where is Mummy?" Akash checked with Aman's mother.

"He is still sleeping. Lazy fellow!" she said with a lot of disappointment and moved to the kitchen.

Akash with the other two boys in the group barged into Aman's room and started creating a ruckus.

"Mummy, see, Daddy has come," Akash said and jumped onto Aman's bed.

Inside the blanket, there were some pillows. Akash was disappointed because Aman was successful in making a fool of him one more time. The other two boys started laughing.

"Stop shouting, guys! Mogambo is at home," Aman said as he stepped out of the bathroom.

The mention of Mogambo was enough to put everyone on mute.

"Hehe… Mogambo has gone to the warehouse," Aman revealed and laughed, pointing a finger at his friends.

They set out for Shimla after breakfast. It took them around nine hours to cover the distance. As planned, they rested and had fun in a hotel room on the first night. The next morning, they went to see different spots. At around 3, they reached an open space near a cliff with nobody in the vicinity. It was kind of a place they wanted to be in. Being artists, they wanted to capture nature on their canvases. They set up everything and started sketching. Each one of the four friends was referencing different directions.

Once Ayush was done with his art, he was excited to show it to his friends.

"Whoa! Look at this, guys. I have created a masterpiece," Ayush expressed excitedly.

It was a usual behavior expected from Ayush. He calls each of his paintings a masterpiece. Hence, no one was interested to see his painting. All were busy with their own creativity.

"Guys, you have to see it before it is too late," Ayush gave a weird signal.

"Before it's too late?! What do you mean by that?" Ghalib curiously asked. The other two friends got irritated.

"You have to see it to understand it," Ayush was desperate to get everyone's attention.

Ghalib got irritated. "What masterpiece have you created? Is it going to disappear…" Ghalib was dumbstruck upon seeing the painting.

"Ya Allah!" he screamed.

The reaction was enough to grab the attention of Aman and Akash as well. They quickly approached to see the masterpiece.

On seeing the painting, the boys were more interested in the direction Ayush was referencing than the painting. Ayush had replicated nature as it was.

"For how long has that girl been standing at that spot?" Aman asked.

"From the time I started drawing. Must have been there even before that," Ayush replied.

"What has she been doing there?" Aman inquired further.

"I think she is mad," Ayush shared his opinion.

"What do you mean?" Ghalib asked.

"For the whole time that I have been observing her, she goes to the edge and then comes back to the rock. She is very anxious and restless. I think she is talking to herself. At times, she screams. Aren't these symptoms of madness?" Ayush checked.

Everyone except for Ayush got worried upon hearing that.

"She is not mad, but you are. Stupid, she has gone there to commit suicide," Aman retorted.

"What!" Ayush reacted. He was the only one shocked by the revelation.

"I am sorry I didn't realize that," Ayush said.

"Hell..." he was about to scream out loud when Aman held his mouth with his hand.

"Have you gone mad? If she comes to know we are here, she may jump off without thinking," Aman said.

"Then, what should we do, mummy?" Akash checked.

"I got an idea. I will go near her stealthily and act as if I want to commit suicide. I think she will realize this is a wrong step through my example," Aman proposed.

"And what should we do? Should we call the police?" Ghalib asked.

"That will be too late. They will come if they need to trace the body. For now, all you three observe us from here. If I am not able to convince her against suicide, I will hold her tight at a distance. When I do that, you all come to help me," Aman described his plan.

"However, if I am successful in convincing her without any physical dominance, you people go back to the hotel. Now, come on. Pack up everything," Aman said and ran towards the girl after quickly grabbing his backpack.

Everyone agreed with Aman's idea. At least, they seemed to have. They quickly packed their stuff and loaded them in the car by the time Aman reached the spot.

On seeing Aman convince the girl and walk back along with her, the three friends got into the car and as decided earlier, left for the hotel room.

"Mummy is such an expert! He has saved a life today," Ayush said in the car.

The other two nodded their heads in agreement.

"But this is just temporary. The girl may jump off tomorrow," Ghalib feared.

"That's not our responsibility. We didn't let anything wrong happen in front of our eyes. So many people commit suicide every day. One more will be added. It doesn't matter. The only thing is that it shouldn't happen in front of us," Akash expressed his notions.

"That's so rude!" Ghalib said with a bit of disappointment.

"That is. But if everyone thinks like me, no suicide will take place. Because every person in the world is being watched by someone or the other. It's their responsibility to stop it from happening," Akash argued as he rotated the steering wheel clockwise and the car took a right turn.

Ayush gave a signal through his eyes to Ghalib not to argue with the driver. That might put everyone's life in danger.

Chapter 3: The Restart

Aman reaches the hotel late in the evening. Even though he has distracted Padma from suicidal thoughts, he is not sure if she is convinced.

"Mummy!" Ghalib screams as Aman enters the room. Aman doesn't respond. He seems to be lost in thoughts.

"What happened, mummy?" Akash asks in a concerned tone.

"It's depressing to see anyone so broken that they decide to take such extreme steps," Aman replies in a low voice as he sits down on the bed and sighs.

"Hey, don't get depressed because of that. You can't help it much. You have done a very good job today. You saved her life," Akash tries to cheer up his friend.

"By the way, any details about her?" Ghalib is curious and so are others.

"She works in Delhi. She is from Andhra. Srikakulam. Her name is Padma," Aman reveals.

"And why was she attempting suicide?" Ayush shows more curiosity.

"She had eloped with her boyfriend three months ago. That guy dumped her, left her alone a couple of days back, and returned to his family. She has nowhere to go now."

"Poor girl," Ghalib says as he takes a deep breath. He realizes something. "Hey, if she stays here, she might attempt suicide again. Why didn't you recommend that she should go back to Delhi?" he inquires.

"I have already proposed it to her. She is going back to Delhi with us tomorrow," Aman reveals.

"With us?"

"With us?"

"With us?"

All three express their concern one after another.

"Yes, with us. Is there a problem?" Aman asks assertively.

Traveling with a girl means compromising many things. They have to watch their tongue and be gender sensitive all the time. They cannot halt at a cheap *dhaba*. They cannot pee by the roadside.

"No, no. No problem as such," Ayush says as they look at each other helplessly.

"I know what you all are thinking. I think we don't need to apply any filters to us. We will be what we are. But of course, we need to refrain from being vulgar," Aman tries to assure his friends.

They don't seem to be assured though.

"You didn't tell us, mummy, how you were able to convince her against suicide," Akash expresses his curiosity.

"I was going to come to that. Good, you asked," Aman gets excited to reveal his trick and boast about his presence of mind.

"As I told you I went there and pretended as if I was going to commit suicide. Naturally, she tried to save me. And, in her bid to convince me, she realized her own mistake," Aman adds.

"But how does it work? And, how come you were so confident? We observed you were looking at ease," Ayush checks.

"Tell me who is the doctor amongst us," Aman asks.

"Akash," Ayush and Ghalib babble.

"Right. So, whenever we fall sick, Akash recommends home remedies, right?"

Nobody responds. Akash doubts if he is going to be the butt of some joke as his name has come up.

"But, last time, when Akash had a sore throat, he was asking for our advice, wasn't he?" Aman asks as he giggles and waits to get responses. He doesn't get any response from his friends as they are all skeptical of him.

"We gave Akash the same suggestion that he would have given us if we had a sore throat," Aman explains.

"So, what do you mean, Mr. Philosopher?" Akash gets a little irritated.

"Not a philosopher. Say, Psychologist. We gain knowledge through different mediums, be it books, teachers, experience, or anything. We help others when they ask for advice. Sometimes, we try to help even when we are not asked for it. However, when we are at the receiving end, we forget our own wisdom," Aman shares a piece of psychology.

"What happened in Padma's case is that she knew suicide was not the solution for her issues. She knew such situations were not the end of the world. But, because she was at the receiving end, she forgot. She just needed someone to make her realize it," Aman continues.

"Am I boring you with too much lecture?" he asks.

"No, no. It's good," Ayush responds.

"Okay. So, when I posed as someone who would commit suicide, Padma argued with me and provided me with the reasons why I shouldn't commit suicide. While doing so, she realized her own mistake. While she was talking to me, she was also talking to herself," Aman concludes his analogy.

All the friends are happy now. The other three feel proud of Aman.

"Mummy, it was such a wonderful presence of mind," Akash confesses as they leave for dinner.

Contrary to the boys' fears, Padma is not thinking about committing suicide anymore. She now wants to prove to the world that she can live by herself. After a couple of days, she had dinner today. However, she has one fear. She feels she should have spent more time with Aman. She is not sure if she was successful in convincing the boy against suicide. What if he changes his mind? She doesn't even know which hotel he is staying in. Otherwise, she could go and check on him.

Padma wants to think positively. She feels stupid that she had suicidal thoughts. In a way, she also thinks Aman saved her. If she hadn't met him at the last minute, she would have jumped off the cliff. Hundreds of thoughts are running through her mind. In a way, it is good for her. It has helped her do away with the angst she has for Venkat.

Both Aman and Padma are not able to sleep. Aman leaves the bed and goes to the garden of the hotel. Coincidentally, Padma does the same thing. They look at the moon from their respective positions.

The moon represents their individual thoughts aptly.

The moon doesn't have its own light. It gets light from the sun. But whatever light it gets from the sun enables the moon enough to help the earth with some light in the dark night. It is Padma's situation. By no means, she is happy now. But she has to give it to Aman as much as she can. She thinks this way she can help him live.

The moon is smaller than the stars. It looks larger and brighter because it's closer to the earth. That's Aman's state of mind now. Even though he doesn't have a lot of ability, he wants to help Padma with all his capacity by staying closer to her, even though it's for a limited time. Padma's situation provides him with a different perspective on life.

As soon as the sun rises, Aman gets ready and steps out of the hotel to meet Padma. He has a different urge to peep into her life.

The sun has not fully come out yet, however, he is too restless to meet Padma. He reaches the hotel and checks with the receptionist about her room number.

"Sir, Padma ma'am has already checked out," replies the boy, rubbing his eyes.

"What!" Aman is both shocked and concerned.

"Can you check if there is any other girl named Padma still staying here?" he requests.

The boy gets a little irritated but comes back to his calm self when Aman offers a fifty-rupee currency note.

"No, sir. I checked the entire register. There is no one else named Padma. Padma ma'am who checked out today was about 5 feet 4 inches, had long hair, wore huge earrings, had a brown complexion. Spoke in a South Indian accent. Are you looking for her?" The boy tries to help Aman in return for the money he received.

"Yes, so she has checked out," Aman says and walks out of the hotel.

He is now worried. Where would she go? Did she go to the railway station? Or, to the cliff again? Numerous thoughts run through his mind. He gets anxious. Suddenly, he recalls he has Padma's phone number. He quickly gives her a call.

"*The number you have dialed is switched off. Please call after some time*," plays on Aman's phone.

Disappointed with himself, he kicks a cold drink can lying on the road. The can hits a trolley bag standing at a distance. Aman is now sorry about his actions. He is about to say "sorry" to the owner of the bag when he realizes it's Padma.

"Hey, what are you doing here? Why did you check out so early?" He checks with Padma.

"I was worried about you. I thought you would attempt suicide again. I couldn't sleep the whole night thinking about you. But I couldn't check with you last evening about the hotel you are staying in. Otherwise, I would have gone there," Padma says.

Aman immediately looks at the phone she is holding.

"I could have called you, but it was too early in the morning. And after I checked out, my phone got switched off," she explains her situation.

Aman feels guilty about his act. He wants to reveal the truth to Padma. However, maybe it's not the right time yet. How does it matter? Once they reach Delhi and he drops Padma off, he is not going to meet her again. So, it doesn't matter what she is thinking about him now. Let her keep thinking that she has saved a life and feel proud of herself. That's the remedy for her depression at the moment.

"Let's go," Aman says as he drags the bag on its wheels to the car and keeps it in the dickey. Like a gentleman, he opens the front door of the car for Padma. They reach the hotel in a few minutes.

Outside the hotel, Aman asks Padma to be in the car and goes to the room to call his friends. No one has got up yet.

"Guys, that girl... Padma is here. We should leave now," he says loudly. When nobody responds, Aman starts requesting each of them.

One by one, all three leave the bed and freshen up. The boys seem to be upset with Aman. They drag themselves along with their bags and other stuff to the car.

Padma gets off the car when the boys reach.

"Let me introduce you all. She is Padma. As I told you I met her last evening near the cliff. And,

Padma, they are my friends, Akash, Ayush, and Ghalib," Aman completes the formality.

From the first appearance, all the boys gauge that Padma is very uncomfortable. This way, the journey back home is going to be really boring.

"Mummy told us about you last night. You are a brave girl" Akash says to cheer her up in his attempt to break the ice.

"I am sorry, who is mummy? And why do you think I am brave?" Padma asks two questions.

"Ah, this guy is popularly known as mummy," Akash points a finger at Aman.

Padma is a little amused, but she tries not to laugh. Aman is already depressed. Any form of embarrassment is not good for him.

"And why do you think I am brave?" She repeats her second question.

Akash doesn't know what to say. He looks at Aman to rescue him.

"I told them that you are living in Delhi alone, working and earning the bread and butter for your family back in Srikakulam," Aman clarifies while clearing his throat.

His gestures work in both ways. For Akash, it means, "Shut up!" And, for Padma, it means, "Please don't mind!"

Aman takes the driver's seat and Padma takes the seat next to him. All three boys take the back seat.

Aman decides to stay serious as for Padma, he is a guy who attempted suicide yesterday.

Padma decides to sound happy as she thinks, for Aman, she is a positive person and not depressed.

The three boys in the back seat are not able to decide how to behave.

After an hour's journey, they halt at the *Dhaba*. It's breakfast time.

As they get down from the car, Akash gives up.

"This can't go like this," he screams.

"What?" The rest of the boys ask while Padma gives an awkward look.

"Padma! Let me tell you. We are all artists. None of us has a girlfriend. And, we have minimum female interaction," Akash pauses as Aman gives him signals to stop.

"No, I will continue. So, can I ask you for something?" Akash asks Padma in a humorous tone.

"What?" she says, wondering how weird the boy is.

"We have eight hours left in our journey. For these eight hours, can we assume you are a boy so we can behave ourselves?" Akash moves his hand on his mustache when he utters 'a boy'. He doesn't have one, so it looks funny.

"Because I think it will be difficult for us to assume we are girls," Akash walks like a girl when he utters 'girls'. It is definitely funny.

Padma starts laughing. She laughs her heart out.

This makes the situation lighter. The boys realize even laughter has an accent.

"You can be whatever you want to be. Why don't you do something? Assume that I am not there. How about it?" Padma gives a solution.

It breaks the ice. They eat well at the dhaba and then continue their journey.

The rest of the journey goes well. Padma, who has got swollen eyes and a sore throat, starts complaining that her jaws are hurting.

"You people are such jokers," she says as she gets down outside her building in Delhi.

"Thanks for the compliment, ma'am," Akash says as Aman drives the car away slowly.

Aman drops everyone off before reaching home. However, the Padma episode doesn't seem to have ended. He is not sure if he has done enough for her to conclude he has performed his social duties. He spends the entire evening on the balcony.

When the thoughts bother him too much, he picks up his phone and attempts to send a message to Padma. But what should he write to her? What right does he have to send her a message? The deal is over now. She saved his life, and he dropped her home. If she asks him not to bother her, it will be quite embarrassing. Numerous questions are there, and none of them has an answer.

"What happened, dear? All good? You look lost," his mother checks with him.

"All good, mummy. No worries," Aman says and decides to put a full stop to Padma's episode here.

Somehow, Aman spends the night on the bed, looking at the ceiling fan and the phone in turns. In the morning, he finally decides to send her a message. It doesn't matter what she thinks. He has to check with her how she is.

"*How are you, Padma? Hope all is well with you,*" he types on his phone, thinks over it for around five minutes, and then finally taps the Send button.

No response. In two minutes, he gets the read receipt. Still, no response.

"*Maybe it doesn't matter to her at all. I am nobody for her. Why will she even bother to reply to me?*" he thinks.

Negative thoughts continue to dominate Aman's mind, but then, his phone vibrates. He quickly checks it. Yes, he has received a message from Padma.

"*I am good till now… got into a little trouble… my brother has come here… he wants to take me to Srikakulam tomorrow,*" he reads the message.

"*Should I call you? I need to talk to you,*" Aman writes without thinking much.

"*No, I can't talk. Came to the washroom to send you the message. But you please dont commit suicide,*" she writes.

"No, no. I won't. I am happy for you. Finally, you are going home."

"This is not good news. They have filed a case against Venkat. Now, they want me to go there and testify that he had kidnapped me."

"Oh, that's bad. What will you do now?"

"No idea."

Aman doesn't know what to write now. He shouldn't have sent the first message to her. Now, he is even more disturbed than before. Till noon, he stays away from his phone but then he feels like checking with her.

"So, you don't want to go back to Srikakulam, do you?" he sends.

"No. But I have no choice. My brother will forcibly take me with him," he receives after 10 minutes.

"Why don't you flee?" he sends.

"How will I do that? He is watching me all the time. And where will I go after fleeing?" he receives.

"I will have a solution for that. But you flee if you want to and then call me," he sends.

He doesn't receive any response till the evening. Now, he thinks the chapter is closed. Padma will go to her hometown and accept her fate. Why should it bother him? There are so many Padmas in our country. He cannot make an impact on everyone's life.

To calm down his restless brain, Aman takes the brush and starts painting. It is less of painting and more of venting out on the canvas.

At around 8 pm, when Aman is still painting, he gets a call, which he ignores. He is not yet done with venting out. When it continues buzzing, he picks up the phone and speaks angrily.

"Hello!"

Immediately after speaking, he realizes it is Padma at the other end. She hasn't spoken yet. His subconscious mind sends the message to his conscious mind but a bit late.

"I have fled from the flat," says Padma.

Aman is spellbound. His voice is choked. He wants to speak but is not able to.

"Are you still alive? Or have you committed suicide?" she asks. There is sarcasm in her words but not in her tone. Her tone reflects sadness.

"Yes, I am very much alive. Where are you?"

"Outside R K Puram Metro Station."

"My home is in Vasant Vihar. It will take me five minutes only. You please stay there. I am leaving now," Aman says as he heads to the parking area after picking up the keys to his car.

He is about to leave his room when his mother checks with him, "Where are you going? Not having dinner at home today?"

"I will bring a friend home, mummy. We will have dinner together. Mummy, can you clean my room please?" he says before leaving for his mission.

Aman's room is normally neat and clean. He maintains it well. 'Cleaning' means keeping the painting on the shelf.

The artist's mother is stunned when she looks at the painting he has created. It's a girl trapped in a cage. Several people representing the society are standing around her. They are all pointing fingers at her, laughing. The girl dares look into their eyes. Though tears roll down her cheeks, she hasn't broken down. The artist hasn't drawn anyone's face other than that of the girl clearly. On seeing the kind of agony the painting exhibits, Aman's mother feels like crying. She feels empathetic to the girl though it is just a picture.

Anyway, as requested by her son, she keeps the painting on the shelf. She feels proud of him. She has raised him well. *"A boy who empathizes with a woman is a gentleman,"* she thinks.

In 10 minutes, Aman reaches the R K Puram Metro station. He doesn't have to struggle much to find Padma. 'Standing near the ticket counter' is sufficient input for him to trace her.

They reach home in another 15 minutes.

"Do you think it's okay for me to go to your home? Will your parents not have any issues?" Padma asked on the way.

"No. Mogambo, I mean, my father is in his own world. He is always into business and keeps himself busy counting money. My mother is a gem of a person. She is waiting for you. We will have dinner together," Aman explained.

Suman, Aman's mother, just keeps staring at Padma as she enters the house and seeks her blessing by touching her feet.

Aman has brought his female friends home before as well. So, bringing a girl is not a reason for the weird reaction. Padma is the girl in the painting. Aman realizes his mother must have seen the painting. He keeps his hands on her shoulder and talks through his eyes. Suman seems to have understood a lot of things from this non-verbal communication. She holds Padma's hand and takes her inside.

"Go, freshen up. We will have dinner," she tells Padma.

Following dinner, Suman, Padma, and Aman have a discussion. Padma reveals everything about her except for the suicide episode. She tells them that Venkat has given all her whereabouts to the police. Her family now wants her to go to Srikakulam and tell the police that Venkat kidnapped her. She ran away when her brother went to the washroom. That was the only opportunity she could get. Now, she cannot go back to the flat and even cannot go to the office she is working at. Padma has switched off her phone to keep anyone from contacting her.

Suman recommends that she should stay at their place for a few days. Though Padma doesn't look very comfortable, Suman's affection overpowers the discomfort. As it is, she doesn't have an alternative plan now. Going with the flow seems to be the only plan left.

The doubt that Padma has now is why a boy like Aman would attempt suicide. He has such a lovely family. He seems to be happy and mentally very strong. Why would such a person even get depressed about a girl? It's hard for her to digest. Anyway, she has reserved the question for another occasion.

Chapter 4: The Reveal

Padma gets up in the morning early, freshens up, and goes to the kitchen as she finds Suman there.

"Good morning, aunty!"

"Good morning! You got up so early?"

"Yes, I normally get up at this time. Do you get up so early every day?"

"Yes, your uncle is an early bird. He needs breakfast early. Then, we won't see him the whole day."

"Aunty, does uncle know about me?" Padma checks.

"Yes, I told him last evening, but of course, not everything. He knows what he needs to know," Suman says as she takes the *paratha* out of the pan and puts it on the plate.

"I will go and give it to Mogambo, I mean, your uncle. Can you make one more *paratha* by the time," Suman says and leaves the kitchen with the plate.

The bell rings now.

"Uma, please see who is at the door," Suman calls out to the maid from the dining room.

Within a minute, Ayush enters the kitchen.

Ayush hadn't slept the whole night. He wanted to show his masterpiece to Suman who always thinks Aman is a much better artist. He has argued with Suman many times in the past about this but never gets tired of it.

"You will always take your son's side, aunty," he says whenever he loses an argument.

That line never fails. "You are also my son," is Suman's usual response.

Today is a different day though. Ayush thinks he has an edge today. For the first time in his life, he can prove his superiority over Aman as an artist.

"Aunty, look at this. Tell me how it is!" Ayush screams as he unrolls the painting.

His mouth stays open for a while as Padma turns around and looks at the painting. This is something he didn't expect. The painting is not meant for Padma to see either. Padma is as tall as Suman and is wearing one of Suman's maxis. That's one of the reasons Ayush couldn't see it coming. However, he should have paid attention to the hair. Padma has it till her waist and Suman till her shoulder.

Someone taps Ayush on his shoulder from behind. He comes back to his senses and finds Suman as he turns around.

"Aunty…!" He can hardly speak now. He quickly rolls back the painting.

Suman gauges the situation. This guy has got the shock of his life on seeing Padma in the kitchen.

In two minutes, Suman and Ayush meet in Aman's bedroom.

"How come she is here, aunty?" Ayush asks as soon as they enter the room.

On hearing the noise, Aman gets up and joins the conversation. He is now worried about explaining it to Padma. Suman doesn't know that Padma was about to commit suicide. She is not able to guess it from the painting even now.

But Padma was under the impression that she saved Aman's life and that Aman had no idea of her suicide plans. From the painting, she must have guessed that Aman already knew about it, which means Padma didn't keep Aman from suicide. On the contrary, Aman did it for Padma.

While all this is going on in Aman's mind, Ayush is busy trying to prove to Suman that his artwork is better than anything Aman has created by now.

"Look at the details, aunty. This is Padma, and she is looking at the valley from the cliff. Do you see the details?" Ayush continues to convince her. He thinks his painting is out of this world. Nobody can create a masterpiece like this. He has created it within an hour; that's a great level of efficiency.

Suman listens to his argument for a few minutes. She doesn't say a word. She has something in mind but wants to listen to Ayush carefully, so he doesn't complain later.

"Look at the bird sitting on the rock, aunty. Every minute detail is captured in this painting," he continues his argument.

"You are not saying anything. Are you spellbound by this piece of art, aunty?" Ayush checks with a lot of confidence as he rests his case.

Suman now gets up. She walks out of Aman's room. Ayush doesn't understand her reaction.

"What happened to her, mummy? Is she going to bring a prize to give me?" Ayush checks with Aman who is still sitting on the bed thinking about how to explain it to Padma.

In a minute, Suman comes back with another painting. She unrolls it and puts it in front of Ayush's face. Unlike Ayush, she doesn't need words to present her case. She has profound evidence, a picture that has the ability to speak for itself. They say a picture is worth one thousand words. In this case, it is numerous.

Ayush is awestruck. It's the same Padma. Just her face. A lot of fingers pointing at her. One can feel her agony as well as her strength and courage. She is suppressed by her own people but dares stand against them and society. The painting emotes both extreme expressions at the same time. Though one can see tears on her cheeks and her eyes wet, it seems like a volcano has erupted and she is releasing lava through her eyes.

Ayush, who stood up to see the painting, takes a seat on the bed. He doesn't need to say anything. His acceptance of defeat is quite obvious.

"Yours is not bad, Ayush. But do you see what Aman created? What you created replicates what was there in front of you, but what he created goes beyond representational and metaphorical and tells a lot of things without actually telling them. Do you get my point?" Suman asks.

"I agree," Ayush replies.

Padma knocks on the door.

"Should I serve breakfast for everyone, aunty?" she says from the door itself.

"Yes, dear," Suman replies. She then tries to wake up her son, "Aman, come on, get up. All the artists will have breakfast together."

Still struggling to decide how to face Padma's questions, Aman hesitates to leave the bed. But somehow, he has to do it.

At the dining table, Aman avoids eye contact with Padma. Ayush focuses on the *parathas*. What else can be better for a defeated artist than to find solace in food?

"Why don't you sit with us, Padma?" Suman asks Padma as she doesn't take her seat.

"Aunty, you said, the artists will have breakfast together. I am not an artist," Padma makes a sad face. Her voice is still hoarse.

"Ah! You are feeling bad about that. Do you watch movies? Do you listen to songs? Do you like paintings?" Suman asks.

"Yes, I like movies and songs," Padma replies.

"So, do you appreciate good movies or songs?" Suman asks.

"Yes, aunty," Padma responds.

"Then, you are an artist. I was reading a book called '14 Nights & The Wedding Gift' yesterday. One of the characters says, 'One who appreciates good art is no less than an artist.' That makes you and me artists," Suman says as she pulls Padma by her hand.

"No one can beat aunty in an argument," Ayush says looking at Padma while relishing a bite of *paratha*.

Aman is the only one here who is not talking at all.

"So, aunty, even Aman delivers beautiful lines. Is it you from whom he has picked up the skill?" Padma checks with Suman but looks at Aman.

"He is a true artist. He thinks from his heart. I don't think I can teach him anything," Suman looks at Padma as she replies. However, she notices something fishy. Padma is looking at Aman. Aman is not making eye contact with her. There is something she doesn't know.

These are situations that Suman wants her son to face and handle. It will make him mature and emotionally stronger. In the past, she has let Aman deal with so many issues on his own. However, such matters are very delicate. These are matters of life and death. Aman is finding it difficult to get out of it.

Suman decides to wait and watch. She will make an entry only if things go out of control for the kids.

After breakfast, Ayush leaves like a retreating army after defeat. He is determined to come back stronger, which is not something unusual.

Aman takes refuge in paintings, so he doesn't have to face Padma. Padma takes refuge in cooking, so she doesn't have to think about her future and past. Suman keeps herself busy by reading novels.

However, it can't go like this. Human beings are not like this. There are three people under one roof. They can't go without talking for a long time, particularly the women.

After lunch is prepared, Padma decides to take a tour of the house. They are rich, no doubt. But it's not a bungalow. It's a flat. A three-bedroom flat. In 20 seconds, Padma ends up in Aman's room. She knocks on the door before entering. He looks at her but doesn't respond. She takes the silence as 'yes' and enters the room.

Two paintings are lying on the bed. Padma picks the one closest to her. Aman keeps himself busy with the colors and avoids looking at her. He hopes Padma leaves his room soon, but it is not likely to happen. She unrolls the painting in her hand.

It's the same one Ayush displayed in the morning. She recalls how he got shocked to find her in the kitchen. It brings a smile to her face. Then she starts looking at the minute details in the painting. She hadn't observed her surroundings well when she was at the cliff. Her focus was on the valley and on her past. Now she is getting a bird's eye view. The painting shows that there is more to life than just oneself.

The more Padma looks at the painting, the more she feels embarrassed. It looks like the painting allowed her to look at herself and watch her own actions. "What a masterpiece it is," Padma utters.

"Yup. Ayush created it," Aman gives credit to the creator like a true artist.

"Aunty said you also created a masterpiece. Is it this one?" Padma asks as she picks up the other painting lying on the bed.

"It's nothing. Mummy praised me because of her love for me," he tries to sound humble or maybe he is.

That reminds Padma of something she wanted to check with Aman. She was about to unroll the painting, but she pauses there. "Why does everyone call you Mummy? Your name is Aman, isn't it? Is that your nickname?"

Aman can comfortably answer this question. He smiles. Till now, Padma hadn't seen him smile. By general standards, Aman can be described as handsome. But when he smiles, he looks adorable. He doesn't have a strong body, but definitely sports an athletic physique, which is attractive for women.

"You remember that guy Akash?" Aman asks.

"That funny guy on your trip?" Padma checks.

"Yes. He is not funny usually. It was his attempt to cheer you up and make the trip enjoyable. He is my childhood friend. He and I grew up in the same locality. We used to play a lot together,'' Aman realizes something and then stops talking and continues painting. He hopes Padma forgets her question.

"Then?" Padma follows up.

"Then?" he asks back.

"You didn't tell me why they call you mummy," she complains.

Aman has to reveal it now. He cannot distract Padma anymore. She is too curious.

"When we were in primary school, Akash and I used to get engaged in pretend play along with some other children. In the act, I used to pretend as mummy, and he would act as daddy. It started from there and continues till now," Aman says with a little embarrassment.

Padma seems to be amused to know this. She
controls her laughter to avoid being insensitive.
"So, you never mind when they call you that?"
"Why will I? Mothers are the most beautiful
creations on Earth. I wanted to pretend to be a
mother because I liked that role the most. Being
called mummy is not something to be embarrassed
about but to feel proud of. They must have seen
those amazing qualities in me to some extent,"
Aman says and smiles at Padma.

Padma is amazed by this guy. She has never met
someone like him. He is in his mid-twenties but
talks like a mature man.

"Wow! You sound like a great philosopher," she
says.

"Do I?" he asks humbly. "Mummy also says so."

"Yes," says Padma, and then follows an
awkward silence.

Padma looks around the room and realizes she
hasn't looked at what Aman has created.

She unrolls it without further delay.

Aman cannot stop her now. On seeing that she has
already unrolled it, he hides behind the canvas.
When he doesn't hear anything from Padma, he
tries to check if she is there in the room or has left.

She is very much there in the room. Sitting on the
bed, she is just looking at the painting. Her eyes are
stuck to the sight. Aman approaches her to check if
she is fine. She looks at Aman and keeps looking at

him senselessly. Struggling to find a way to handle the situation, Aman holds her by her arms and shakes her.

"Padma, are you fine?"

A stream of tears flows from her eyes and makes their way to her chin, falling from there on her dress. She doesn't bother to wipe them.

"Is it me? Yes, it's me. Where am I standing now? What is this juncture?" Padma keeps questioning herself.

"Everything is fine, Padma. There is nothing to worry about. You will have a new beginning," Aman explains to her.

"Who are you?" Padma asks.

"I am Aman," he replies innocently. He doubts if Padma is in some shock.

"No. Tell me if you are God or a human being. You came from nowhere, pretended to commit suicide, and helped me do away from committing suicide. You then gave me refuge at your home. Who are you?"

Padma breaks down. Her voice is loud enough to have Suman in the room.

Suman comes running into the room and takes Padma in her arms. Aman feels relieved at the moment. The situation was getting out of his hands. His mother reached just in time like an angel.

Chapter 5: The Urge

Aman is a bit more relaxed now. He was wondering how Padma would react if she came to know about the truth. He was finding it difficult to reveal it to her. Luckily, the two paintings did the magic. They say a picture is worth a thousand words. In this case, it is not only worth the words but emotions, fears, and a lot of things.

Suman now knows the truth from Padma. She cannot be prouder of her son. Earlier, she thought that Aman was trying to help a girl in distress. Now, she knows that he also saved her life.

The food habits in this North Indian family have changed now. They have shifted to *idlis* and *dosas* from *parathas* at least for breakfast following Padma's entry.

"Will he join me in the business? I need someone to lend a hand," Mogambo asks as he washes his hands after breakfast.

"He has straightaway refused," Suman responds to her husband.

"Your wish. I hope he does well with paintings then," he says and leaves for work.

Padma hasn't seen Mogambo yet. Her exposure to Mogambo is limited to his voice and what she has heard from others about him. Today, she overheard him talking to Suman.

"Aunty, what business uncle is into?" she asks after Mogambo leaves.

"He is into the tea leaves business. Such a boring business! Tell me how my poor son will manage it. He is an artist," Suman says in a concerned tone.

"Even my father is into the same business," Padma reveals.

Suman is thrilled to know this. She gets an idea.

"Do you find the business boring?" she asks.

"No, no. It's good. I would have joined my father in his business if I hadn't eloped," Padma replies.

"Well, Padma. I have a proposal for you. My husband is looking for someone who can assist him. Will you be able to take up that job?" Suman checks.

Padma doesn't know how to react to it. She has spent a week in this stranger's house. She will do everything to pay off that debt. But this is not a favor she will do for this family. On the contrary, the family is doing a favor for her by offering her a job.

"Don't worry about the salary. You will be paid well. Much more than your earlier job," Suman says as she finds Padma a little hesitating.

"No, no, aunty. Salary is not at all a concern. I can work for free. I am thinking how I will be able to work with Mogambo, I mean, with uncle," Padma expresses her fears.

Suman laughs uncontrollably.

"I am sorry," Padma gets apologetic.

"No, no. No problem," Suman says.

"By the way, why do you call him by that name?" Padma asks out of curiosity.

"Mogambo was the name of a villain in a Hindi movie. The villain was ruthless. He would kill even his loyal employees for no reason. Your uncle is nowhere close to him. On the contrary, he is a gentleman. He doesn't talk much. See, you have been in this house for a week now and he hasn't talked to you yet. That's why we call him by that name," Suman explains.

"Does he know he has this name?" Padma asks.

"Of course, not," Suman giggles and raises both her hands to give a high five. But she withdraws as Padma doesn't reciprocate.

The ladies go shopping in the evening. Padma needs new apparel now. She must be tired of wearing Suman's clothes. Tomorrow onwards, she will go to the office and assist Mr. Arvinder Kirad. She now knows his real name.

If anyone is the happiest in this home now, it is Aman. Mogambo will not bother him anymore by asking him to visit the office.

In the evening when they meet, Aman thanks Padma for this. She doesn't know how to react. Aman, who saved her life, allowed her to stay in his house, gave her a job, and treated her so well that she could overcome such a shock, is thanking her for taking up a job she was offered. What an irony! Do such men exist? If yes, she hasn't met any before. The only man she knew well outside her family, whom she loved more than her life and trusted blindly, has left her to suffer in this unknown city.

"Why are you thanking me? I should thank you," Padma reverts.

"I should thank you because if you had refused to take up this job, Mogambo would have insisted on me taking it up. I wouldn't get time for art if I had to sell tea leaves."

"Ah! I see. In a way, it's good for me. You don't have to worry about me getting the thought of suicide again now that I have a job too. Can you help me find a place to shift to?"

"Why? Aren't you comfortable here?"

"I am. But… you know… I mean…"

"She means she thinks she has become a burden on us," Suman joins the conversation. She has come to the balcony with a tray, which contains three cups of tea and some biscuits. It's tea time.

"No, aunty. I didn't mean that. I am very much comfortable here. But…" Padma hesitates to complete the sentence.

"But? But you can't stay here? Why?" Suman sounds irritated.

Padma doesn't say anything. She has decided to leave this house. That's how it has to be. Too much favor is not good for her health. Now that she has decided to live, she will have to live on her own.

Finding a flat for a single woman is somewhat difficult even though it is not impossible. Aman has been reading about the suicidal tendency. He learns that people who have attempted suicide once may get suicidal thoughts again. Hence, he finds accommodation for Padma in a women's hostel close to Vasant Vihar. At least, she will be surrounded by people all the time.

Padma has been going to the office to assist Mogambo for the last seven days. And today she is moving to the hostel. It's an emotional moment for everyone.

She doesn't have a lot of luggage to carry.

"I will miss you a lot," Suman says with wet eyes.

"She means your *idlis*," says Aman in an attempt to make the situation lighter.

Aman didn't fail in his attempt. The ladies smile.

"I will visit you every Sunday, aunty," Padma says as she leaves. She is accompanied by Aman, who is carrying her bag.

"Why do you women cry all the time?" Aman asks as they walk towards the hostel.

"Because we don't keep it inside like you men."

Aman gets his answer. This woman is too sharp. He shouldn't mess with her.

They walk for a few minutes without talking to each other.

"Will you come to meet me?" Padma checks as the hostel appears in their sight.

"Why not? Every Sunday, I will come and take you home. But not the coming Sunday," he says.

"Why? Are you going somewhere?"

"Going to Hyderabad. There is an art exhibition happening. Our paintings will be a part of it."

The mention of Hyderabad was enough to get a reaction from Padma. Srikakulam is close by from there. Both cities are part of the undivided Andhra Pradesh. People in both cities speak a common language—Telugu.

"What happened?" Aman asks as she is dumbfounded.

"Nothing. I haven't seen my parents for the last four months," she manages to speak.

Aman realizes the proximity of Hyderabad to Srikakulam. He empathizes with her.

"Why don't you come with us? We will go to Srikakulam after the exhibition is over," Aman proposes.

"It's not that close. Will take a lot of time from Hyderabad. And...?

"And?"

"And I can't go to Srikakulam. I can't show my face to them. Have lost my respect in their eyes. They will now spit on my face."

"But Venkat could be accepted!"

"Yeah! He is a boy."

"You both did the same act. You are blamed, he is not. How come!"

"I told you; he is a boy."

Aman gets angry all of a sudden. Padma can see that. She goes inside the hostel with her bag without saying anything.

As Aman walks back, he calls his friends. He needs to talk to them to feel better.

The team gathers in Aman's room in an hour. It's Sunday, and Mogambo is at home. So, they need to watch their volume.

"It's about Padma," Aman starts the conversation.

"Oh no. Not again. I knew it would happen one day. You have fallen for her, haven't you?" Ayush reacts before Aman reveals anything.

"*Bewakufon ki kami nahin hai Ghalib, ek dhoondhon hazaar milte hain* (Poet Ghalib says, there is no scarcity of stupid people. Look for one, and you will get a thousand of them.)" says Ghalib.

"What do you mean?" Ayush asks.

"He means you are stupid," Akash chooses to be direct this time as being poetic didn't work for Ayush last time.

"And it is to be noted that these lines were written by Poet Mirza Ghalib and not by me," Ghalib gives credit to the real poet like a true artist.

Aman has earned a 'no nonsense' image in his friend circle. He must be concerned about something if he has asked everyone to gather here.

After taking a break, Aman describes his conversation with Padma in the morning.

"It will be fun," says Ghalib after hearing the story.

"I mean, traveling to Srikakulam," he explains as the other three stare at him skeptically.

Akash is still in two minds. He doesn't say anything.

"You don't want her to come with us?" Aman checks with Akash.

"No, mummy. I mean I would want her to come with us. Then, we can also see Srikakulam. But if anyone from her family or known to her spots her, we will be in trouble," Akash sounds genuinely concerned.

They break their head on this matter for an hour, and then it's lunchtime. The group has nothing to hide from Suman. They continue their discussion at the dining table.

"I have an idea," Suman says hesitantly.

Nobody pays attention to her. They continue to talk.

"I said I have an idea." She is much louder than the last time. They cannot ignore her now.

"Yes, aunty. What's your idea?" Akash asks without any interest to know the answer.

"Can she cross-dress? I mean, do some makeup, and look different, so nobody recognizes her in Srikakulam," she hesitantly reveals her idea.

On hearing this, all the boys except for Aman give disappointed reactions.

"Yes! It's a good idea. Let's do it," Aman says while the other boys continue overacting.

All three of them look at Aman in disbelief. Akash has a mixed reaction; he is in disbelief as well as frustrated.

Suman feels valued. "See, only a true artist can appreciate my excellent idea," she says.

"Even I like your idea, aunty," Ayush falls into the trap.

"Wait," says Akash. "Do you all think Padma will agree to this weird idea?" He raises a valid question.

"We will try. I will convince her," says Suman confidently. "Everything comes at a price. If she wants to see her parents, she has to do this," she adds.

"And you think it's easy," Akash sounds a little rude this time. But Suman doesn't seem to be upset with him.

"You don't know women, Akash. We can go to any level for our loved ones," she says as she places a chapati on everyone's plates except for that of Akash. She doesn't even look at him. Akash gets the message—Don't mess with Mummy's mummy.

Chapter 6: The Transformation

Padma couldn't manage more than a few hours in the hostel. She missed the Kirad family badly. Therefore, in the evening, she pays a visit.

Suman somehow knew it was going to happen. She was prepared for it. "Come, Padma. We will make rice and rasam today for dinner," Suman says as soon as Padma enters the house.

On her way, Padma kept thinking about an excuse for visiting Suman. With Suman's warm welcome, she doesn't have to give an excuse. She feels at home.

"The boys are going to Hyderabad. Why don't you go with them? You can go visit Srikakulam as well from there," Suman shoots the question as soon as she gets a chance while preparing dinner.

Padma feels a little uneasy. However, she has nothing to hide from Suman.

"I can't visit Srikakulam, aunty," she responds.

"Why? Don't you want to see your parents?"

"I do want to. But they don't want to see me."

"Well, what if you get to see them without them seeing you?"

"How is that possible, aunty?"

"I have an idea. But I fear you won't get the courage to execute it."

The phrase 'won't get the courage' didn't go down well with Padma. "*I almost died a few days ago, and now I am managing on my own. What else does this lady want me to do to prove that I have a lot of courage?*" she thinks. She convinces herself that she will take any challenge Suman throws at her. She cannot afford to lose a challenge and be considered a failure.

"Tell me, aunty. I am ready to take up anything you have in mind. I promise I won't say 'no' to you," Padma says with a smile on her face.

"Be cautious, Padma. You never know. I might ask for your kidney!"

Padma laughs. "I have two of them. I won't think twice before giving one to you," she says without batting an eyelid.

"That's so nice of you. Okay, then, I think you are ready for the challenge... How about dressing up like a boy and going to Srikakulam to see your parents?"

Oops! "*I have overpromised,*" Padma realizes. She now repents of underestimating Suman.

"Exciting, no?" Suman asks.

"How is that possible, aunty?" Padma questions.

"You promised you wouldn't refuse."

"I know, but how is this possible? Aren't you thinking too wild? Such things happen only in movies."

"Leave it to me. We will try out make-up and apparel. If it doesn't look convincing, I won't force you. Does that work?"

Padma doesn't respond. She hopes it doesn't work out. Aman and his friends are artists but not make-up artists. Painting on canvas and painting on a face are two different things. Padma hopes Suman knows this.

At the dinner table, Suman reveals the news to Aman. *"How could mummy convince Padma of this stupid act?"* he thinks. More than that he is surprised by the fact that Padma agrees to the idea.

He tries to make eye contact with Padma but fails. She doesn't look at him. Her eyes are on the plate.

The next day, Aman and his friends meet in his room. Mission 'Transform Padma into a man' begins. Before the actual work, the project will be drawn on a canvas. Ayush draws a portrait of Padma first. Then, the group takes their seats to discuss. Suman is just an onlooker. She doesn't comment. After a brief discussion, they conclude that a thin mustache, light beard, short hair, and dark complexion should work. Ayush goes ahead and makes the changes to the portrait. Apart from the said changes, he proactively removes the nose pin and earrings and broadens the eyebrows.

It doesn't work. That's only the face. Even with pants and a shirt, a woman will look like a woman. Ayush doesn't know how to make modifications to the portrait below the neck. None of the boys know how to do it.

Suman sees them struggling. She finally stands up. "Okay, you people have done your work. I will take care of everything below the neck. Ghalib, can you arrange for the eyebrows and mustache?" she says.

"Yes, aunty. I will get them in the afternoon," Ghalib obliges.

Akash is still not very convinced of the idea. He is the only one disinterested in the whole act. However, he remembers he was not treated well after resisting, hence is keeping mum.

The parlor girl comes home in the evening. She is ready to cut Padma's hair short.

"Can't we manage this with a wig?" Padma looks at the scissors and then looks at her long hair.

"Do you want to take that risk?" Suman says and forces her to take her seat.

The parlor girl starts her job. And she does a decent job.

Padma avoids looking at the mirror. She fears she will not be able to bear the shock.

The only good part about the process is that there is nobody who will laugh at her. She is welcome to take any shape and any appearance. She is unconditionally loved in this home.

After the haircut, she takes a bath and joins Suman and Aman at the dining table for dinner. Aman has already been advised to be indifferent to Padma after the change in appearance so that she feels comfortable. He plays his role perfectly.

"What if it fails?" Padma expresses her doubts while taking a bite of *paratha*.

"It won't," Suman says and goes to Aman's room to bring the painting.

In a few seconds, she comes back.

"See, you will look like this. Do you think anyone will be able to recognize you?" Suman asks while showing her the painting.

"Yeah, but…" Padma still doesn't sound convinced.

Suman and Aman know why she is not. The breasts cannot be concealed. They make her gender quite obvious.

"We will take care of the rest as well," Suman says with confidence without revealing much.

Then onwards, Suman and Aman went shopping every afternoon and try some apparel on Padma every evening.

By Saturday evening, she looks like a man. The feminine assets part is taken care of with a small pillow below them. Padma has also been taught to walk like Akash.

Early in the morning on Sunday, the boys reach Aman's home. They need to leave for the airport. Suman asks everyone to take their seats for breakfast. As she serves them breakfast, a man enters the room and takes his seat next to Akash.

"Oh, my God!" Ghalib reacts.

"This is amazing!" Ayush reacts.

"I mean…" Akash finds it difficult to phrase a sentence.

"I mean…" Padma looks at Akash, imitating him.

"This is awesome!" Akash says.

"This is awesome!" Padma repeats.

Everyone burst into laughter, especially Suman.

After breakfast, Padma goes to the room allocated to her in the house and turns into what she is—a beautiful woman, showing off her curves with a salwar kameez.

"Why did you change? You were looking handsome in that look?" Ayush asks after seeing Padma in female attire.

"Because I am a woman both naturally and in my documents. And the ticket too says I am a woman. If I look like a man, the airport security will smell something fishy and put all of us behind the bars," Padma responds.

Everyone laughs. Ayush feels embarrassed. He is not new to being the butt of a joke. But he didn't expect it from Padma. In his mind, he is repeating, ''Padma, you too!''

Chapter 7: The Adventure

It was a good flight for all of them, particularly for Padma. She had got the window seat. Next to her was Aman. She had a long pending conversation with him.

"It sounds like a movie, isn't it?" Padma started a conversation.

"Yeah. It will be fun. I am sure you will do a good job," said Aman.

"And, I am sure about you," she said.

"I am just a supporting actor here. Don't have much of a role."

"No, I am talking about your painting. You are a great artist."

Aman felt a little uncomfortable. He didn't know how to react. Padma gauged that.

"I wanted to thank you for saving my life," she changed the topic.

"I am glad you are alive."

"Yeah, all because of you. If you hadn't done that stunt that day…" she paused.

"Do you want to know which of my paintings is taking part in the exhibition?" Aman changed the topic.

"No, but every painting of yours is a masterpiece."

"Thanks. That's so kind of you. One request. Please go to the exhibition in your boy's attire."

Padma didn't understand the basis of the request. But she left it to Aman.

"Don't you find it funny?" she said.

"No, you look good. Actually, you look good in any attire," he said and then, thought if he shouldn't have commented on her looks.

Anyway, they had a good journey.

All five men—four real and one fake—reach the exhibition center on time.

During the exhibition, Padma realizes why Aman asked her to come in male attire.

Both Ayush and Aman have put their paintings featuring Padma on exhibition. This doesn't make her uncomfortable. On the contrary, she feels special. She has inspired their art, of course, for all the wrong reasons. During the entire exhibition time, all that she does is wait for it to get over so that they can travel to Srikakulam.

One thing that bothers Ayush throughout the exhibition is that more people gather to see Aman's painting than his. The audience analyzes the painting from different perspectives.

After the exhibition ends, the four boys and the girl impersonating a boy reach the hotel in the evening. And as soon as they reach, Padma runs to the washroom. The men realize she couldn't use the washroom at the exhibition center. In the male attire, she couldn't use the ladies' washroom, nor could she use that of the men. The boys talk amongst themselves and promise each other that they will be more careful about Padma's gender in the future. For the night, they had booked a separate room for Padma, so she sleeps comfortably. Padma was unaware of that and got pleasantly surprised when she learned about it. It's going to be a mixed bag of emotions for her tomorrow. Excitement! Fear! Happiness! Realization! All emotions at a time make it difficult for her to get sleep.

Early in the morning, they set out for their journey to her hometown—a journey of hopes, suspense, excitement, and uncertainty. They have booked a car for the purpose.

It's a 9-hour journey, and Akash thinks he will be bored if he doesn't talk. He doesn't have to work hard to imagine now. Padma has turned into a boy. She is in character, imitating every single move of Akash, following Suman's advice.

Akash takes a look at everyone. "Guys, let's play a game," he screams from the back seat, so it reaches the front seat on which Ayush is sitting. "Now, what game can we play in this tiny car?" Ayush complains.

"Anything that everyone can play in the car," Ghalib says.

"Now, don't say, Antakshari or Dumb Charades," Ayush continues to become the spoilsport. He sounds irritated.

"No, I won't be able to play Antakshari because I don't know many Hindi songs and you people don't know Telugu songs," Padma expresses her concerns.

The driver applies the brake suddenly and looks at Padma in the mirror.

"Speed breaker, sir!" he says as everyone looks at him.

The driver realizes it's not a group of all-boys. The one with a mustache is actually a girl. He glances at all of them to find out who else is a girl.

"We will play Truth or Dare," Akash proposes.

"Oh! How can we play that in this car?" Ayush interrupts.

"You don't play. Look through the window and see which piece of nature you can replicate in your paintings," Akash taunts.

This is enough for Ayush to shut his mouth. Akash's words not only reach his brain through his eardrums, but they also pierce his heart.

Akash realizes his mistake. He shouldn't hurt his friend this way. They all know how much he is struggling with his creativity and approach. However, nothing can be done now. Spoken words and arrows spent from a bow cannot be recalled. One can only compensate for that, which Akash decides to do later.

"I have another idea. May I propose?" Aman asks.

"Yes, mummy. Please go ahead," says Akash.

"Padma is new in our group. She doesn't know much about us. She can pose questions to all of us. We will need to answer those questions. But mind it. She can ask any question. Those who cannot answer her question or don't want to are out. How does that sound?" Aman checks.

Ghalib and Akash agree with the idea. Ayush doesn't respond.

"Padma, do you agree?" Ghalib checks with her.

"Yes, but I don't know what to ask you people."

"Till we reach Srikakulam, you will be restless. You need something to engage your mind. We will cross the bridge when it comes. So, ask us anything that comes to your mind. Who knows? You can find a goldmine from one of us," Aman persuades her.

Padma sees a valid point in Aman's proposal. She is restless at the moment as countless thoughts are running through her mind. All the boys now understand Aman's intent. That's the reason why he is considered the wisest in the group. Even Ayush realizes that now. "Yes, ask your first question to me. I don't have a problem answering any questions. I am an open book," Ayush's voice is louder than ever.

"Okay, here it goes. Ayush, why don't you keep a mustache?"

"Because I don't like hair under my nose; it's as simple as that. Do you like boys with mustaches? Yeah, I know. All your famous Telugu movie actors have huge mustaches," Ayush sounds like he is talking to himself.

"That's not true. I like Mahesh Babu, and he doesn't keep a mustache. That doesn't mean I don't like people with mustaches. Venky..." Padma pauses as she realizes she was speaking what she was not supposed to.

"Hey Ayush, you are not supposed to ask her questions but answer her questions," Akash scolds Ayush for breaking the rule of the game.

Ayush, as usual, realizes his mistake and decides to keep mum. It's Aman's turn now.

"So, Aman, why didn't you get into your father's business?"

"I think one shouldn't sell a product that they don't like. I don't like to consume tea. So, I didn't want to sell tea leaves. My mother says I am an artist. I don't want to lose an artist to tea leaves."

"Wow! What a befitting reply, mummy!" Akash praises his best friend and pats his back, which makes Ayush almost break into tears.

It's Akash's turn now.

"You and Aman used to pretend-play daddy and mummy respectively in your childhood. Would you marry Aman if he was a girl?"

"No! He is too intelligent for me. I would like to marry someone dumb, I mean, less intelligent than me," Akash corrects his choice of word for a woman. But that's okay. Nobody seems to be upset with him.

"Ghalib, are you upset you are the odd one in this group?"

"Odd one, meaning?" Ghalib thinks Padma is indicating his religion.

"Meaning… you are the only one whose name doesn't start with the letter 'A' in this group," Padma clarifies.

"It never struck me. I should feel special about that. But, as Shakespeare says, what's in a name?" Ghalib becomes dramatic in his response.

"Your hearts should match. What say?" Ghalib adds to his answer.

"Yes," Aman reacts.

"Yes," Akash seconds.

"Correct," Ayush agrees.

"That's true," says the driver, and then, realizes he is not part of the game.

"Are we done now?" Padma asks as she has asked her questions to all four boys.

"No, no. Keep asking until you are tired or until we halt for breakfast," Aman proposes.

Ayush eagerly waits for Padma to ask him a question. Hence, he welcomes Aman's proposal. It seems he enjoys the 'Interview' game. It makes him feel like a star.

"Okay. What do you like about your group, Ayush?"

Ayush takes some time to answer this question. He doesn't want to say anything insensible again, which would give Akash a chance to scold him.

"That we all are true artists. That we have a passion for painting. And, that we are all wonderful human beings."

"Awe...." everyone reacts to Ayush. He doesn't make eye contact with anyone to save embarrassment.

It's Aman's turn again, and Padma doesn't want to waste this opportunity. She takes some time to think about it. As she taps her index finger on her chin, Aman waits for the question eagerly.

"What qualities would you like to see in your wife?" Padma spots a naughty smile on her face while asking the question. The feminine smile with the mustache is a rare sight for any man.

Aman is embarrassed now. He didn't see this coming.

"She should be like Ayush's paintings and not like those of mine," Aman answers after giving it a good thought.

"What?!" Padma reacts.

Ayush is now curious to know what Aman means. He cannot afford multiple insults in a single journey.

"Ayush's paintings are direct, straightforward, and hence are easy to understand. I create abstract paintings. They are complex, subjective, and left to viewers' interpretations. I wish I could paint like Ayush," Aman explains.

Ayush, who was paying attention to every word of Aman, now looks at the road. He is done for today. After a long time, someone praised his approach. He can now take numerous jokes on him.

Padma takes a look at Ayush. He is comfortable, relaxed, and at peace. In a few seconds, she revisits all her interactions with Aman in her mind. And, what's the result? At the moment, if anyone asks Padma what traits she would look for in her husband, she will call out every trait Aman poses. He knows how to treat women and make even a stranger girl comfortable. He knows how to make his friends happy. He makes his mother feel proud

of him. He is humane. He is a true artist in every
single way. For the moment, he looks like 'love' to
her. She keeps staring at him.

Before Padma gets lost in her inner world, Ghalib
interrupts.

"Now, it's Akash's turn," he says. As Padma
comes back to her senses, she feels a little weird.
How dare she think of Aman in that manner! This
will be a disservice to his favor. He is her savior,
and he should be considered her savior forever.
Padma shouldn't expect anything more from Aman
or his family. She is indebted to the family. She will
never be able to return the favors in her life.

"Oh, okay. Let me think. Here it goes. So, Akash,
have you ever fallen for a girl?" she asks without
giving it much thought.

Ghalib starts coughing. Ayush prefers to continue
focusing on the road. Aman starts scratching his
forehead. Akash looks uncomfortable.

"Ask him some other question," Aman proposes.

"No, that's against the rule. I should answer this
question too," Akash takes the challenge.

Padma realizes there is something controversial in
the question.

"No, I can change the question," she proposes.

"I was in a relationship with a classmate in our
Art college. Her name is Natasha. She broke up
with me because she had to marry a guy of her
father's choice," Akash says in a hoarse tone.

Everyone's mood suddenly changes. It's pin-drop silence in the car.

Padma realizes why the boys don't have any female friends. They don't seem to be gay either. Maybe they are scared to get into relationships after the bitter experience Akash has gone through.

"Okay. It's Ghalib's turn now," Akash says loudly and excitedly, rubbing his hands together. He probably intends to cheer everyone up.

"What do you like to do except for painting?" Padma asks a simple question to Ghalib to avoid any more complications.

"I do read and write Urdu poetry."

On hearing this, all the boys nod their heads and say, "Irshaad." It's an expression made to request a poem. Padma understands the signal as well. She has seen people in the call center she used to work using such expressions.

"Okay, here is what poet Maharana G says…"

"*Tujhse koi shikwa nahin*
Juda hun par main khafa nahin
Do dil jo bheege the kabhi
Fuharon ka kasoor tha…"

"And what does it mean?" Padma asks. "Sorry, I don't know Hindi or Urdu," she adds.

"Okay, let me try to translate. The poet says, I don't have any complaints against you. Our paths are different, but I am not upset with you. It was the fault of our stars that we fell for each other."

The verses address the situations of both Padma and Akash. Both of them have faced betrayal in love and are dealing with it silently.

On that note, they halt for breakfast at a restaurant.

This journey gives Padma an opportunity to know about each of Aman's friends. She comes to know that Aman and Akash are childhood friends, but Ghalib and Ayush met them in the Art college. She comes to know that Ghalib has one brother, Ayush has one sister, and Akash doesn't have any siblings just like Aman. All the boys are from affluent families. It's okay for their parents for them to take up art as a career even if they don't make any money or become famous. They can afford it.

They cover the rest of the journey in five hours and at around 3 pm, they take a halt at a restaurant on the outskirts of Srikakulam where they plan to have lunch.

Padma lets the boys know that she doesn't feel like eating anything. She sounds nervous. The boys understand the situation. It's natural for her to get nervous.

However, she helps the boys choose items from the menu. She has come to this restaurant many times in the past—sometimes with Venkat and sometimes with other friends.

Padma fears the cashier in the restaurant may recognize her. If that happens, they should take a U-turn from here because then every known person may recognize her.

As the boys are done with lunch, they leave the restaurant. Padma walks swiftly avoiding any eye contact with the cashier. She takes out her handkerchief and wipes the sweat on her forehead and then keeps it back in her pocket.

At that moment, the cashier shouts, "Excuse me." Padma stops. She thinks they are done here. The impersonation is not working. Aman asks her not to move.

"What happened?" he asks the cashier from a distance.

"Nothing, sir. That sir with the mustache has dropped his handkerchief here," he says pointing at the floor.

Aman picks up the handkerchief from the floor. It's a ladies' handkerchief. Hence, he quickly hands it over to Padma before anyone realizes it. They get into the vehicle and start planning what's next.

Padma is now a little more confident that nobody will be able to recognize her. The backup plan is that they will have the vehicle parked close by all the time. In the event of anyone recognizing Padma, they will get into the vehicle and flee from Srikakulam.

They check into a hotel in the evening. The next morning is going to be adventurous.

" Ha Ha. What the hell are we doing? We are artists and now getting into trouble. It feels exciting," Ayush speaks his mind after dinner.

"Are you scared, Ayush? If we get caught, they may tie us to a pole and beat us up till we pass out," Akash says. "You know how it happens in the South Indian movies, right?" he adds to scare Ayush.

It seems he is successful in his attempt. Ayush looks slightly scared.

"Don't worry. My family is not violent. They won't beat me up even if they catch me. They will just disown me," Padma tries to make everyone comfortable. "And Akash, it doesn't happen only in South Indian movies. It happens in those made in the North as well," she becomes defensive.

"But what they show in South Indian movies is different. They take a sword and kill everyone," Ghalib expresses his fear.

"That's a misrepresentation of the society. Movies are only for entertainment. Don't take them seriously and don't worry. I will be more concerned about you all than I will be about myself," Padma assures the boys. She sounds like a mother to them.

Women are like chameleons in a very positive sense. They can change their roles when needed quite easily. They are many in one.

As planned, the boys and the girl go to bed a little early because they need to start the day early tomorrow.

Chapter 8: No Grudges

The next morning, they reach the fields and start capturing the paddy fields in their paintings while the workers are busy farming. They have taken permission from the workers to do so. Although Padma maintains a distance from the workers, nobody seems to have an iota of doubt that she is a woman. They come to know from the workers that the owner of the fields is going to arrive at around 8 am. They have two hours till then and hence focus on their paintings.

Ayush, as expected, makes the best painting. He copies the scenery as it is. Others just pretend to paint.

At around 8, a bald man walks towards the fields. Padma is super nervous. Who can that be? She hardly dares look in the direction the man is coming from.

"Who are you all?" the man in his fifties asks the boys.

"Sir, we are artists. We want to capture this scenery on our canvases. I hope that is fine with you. We took permission from the workers. Are you the owner of these fields, sir?" Akash asks, pointing at one side of the fields.

"No, not that side. The fields on this side are mine. You can do whatever you want to do on those fields," says the bald man.

Padma, observing the conversation from a distance, figures out that the bald man is Appa Rao, Venkat's father.

In a minute, Appa Rao enters the fields and shouts at the workers. As he is doing so, another bald man walks towards the fields.

"It's my father," Padma whispers.

"Okay, we will manage it. You don't worry. Go and pretend like assisting Ayush," Aman says and walks towards the man.

"Who are you all? What are you doing here?" Padma's father asks Aman.

"Sir, we are artists. We have an assignment from our college to create a painting of paddy fields. We took permission from your workers. They were fine with it. Hope you are fine with it," Aman responds.

"But none of you are painting. Only that guy is doing it. Has he done any work yet or just rubbing the brush against that board? Let me see," he says and moves towards Ayush.

Padma slowly walks away from Ayush.

"Wonderful! What a painting!" Padma's father expresses himself loudly as he looks at Ayush's work-in-progress painting.

Ayush is so exhilarated that he starts dancing. He is on cloud nine. And why won't he be? At last, he finds a true fan.

"Where are you all from?" Padma's father asks.

"We are from Delhi. My name is Aman. He is Akash. He is Ghalib. He is Ayush," Aman introduces everyone.

They all say, "Hello, uncle!"

"My name is Srinivas… K Srinivas. I own this piece of land," he stops as he realizes another boy is standing at a distance, who is not introduced.

"Is that guy with you?" he asks, pointing at Padma.

"Yes, uncle. He is not a painter. He assists us. His name is Aditya," says Aman.

Padma refrains from opening her mouth. She just folds her hands to greet Mr. Srinivas.

Appa Rao observes the group on the ridge from his fields. He regrets not befriending the boys earlier. Srinivas seems to have scored against him, which he doesn't like at all. But now, it's too late.

Srinivas looks at Appa Rao. The latter's envy is quite clear. To make his enemy more jealous, Srinivas tries to become even more friendly with the boys.

"So where are you all from, you said?" he asks
Aman loudly so Appa Rao can hear him.

"Sir, Delhi."

"How come you all came so long for painting
then?"

"We had come to Hyderabad for an art exhibition.
Someone told us we will get to see good rice fields
here. So, we came here."

"Even from Hyderabad, it is too far. Looks like
you people are too enthusiastic about painting."

"Yes, sir. Don't you gauge that from my superb
painting," Ayush pitches in.

Akash talks to Ayush through his eyes. The latter
gets the meaning of that gesture. It means, "Can you
please shut up?"

Srinivas looks at Ayush with a smile. He is
already impressed with the boy. "So, what do you
do for a living?" he checks with Aman.

"Nothing else, sir. We put colors on the canvas.
That's it."

"Do you manage to earn your livelihood from
this?"

"No, sir. We don't earn much currently. We are
just learning now. All our parents are
businesspeople. They have earned a lot of money
for us. Now, they want us to become what they
could not become, artists."

Now, Srinivas is not talking to Aman to make his
enemy jealous. His questions are surfacing out of

curiosity. He likes the way Aman is answering his questions.

"What does your father do, Aman? Is that your name?" Srinivas asks.

"Yes, sir. My father is into the tea leaves business."

"Even I am into the tea leaves business. Farming is just for fun."

"Is it? We have a small shop in Chandni Chowk in Delhi."

"Our stuff also comes from Chandni Chowk. There is a wholesaler named Arvinder Kirad. He sends us stuff. Do you know him?"

Aman is awestruck. All the boys and the girl look at him. They don't know if Aman should reveal his identity now. Aman analyzes the situation quickly.

"Yes, sir. I know Mr. Arvinder Kirad very well. He is my father," Aman says after doing the risk analysis in his mind.

"What? You are Mr. Kirad's son!" a pleasantly surprised Srinivas utters.

"Yes, sir," Aman confirms.

"What a pleasant surprise! What a small world it is! I talk to your father once every week but of course, only about business. He doesn't talk much. Is he this way at home as well?"

"Yes, sir. He is a man of few words."

Padma gets unforgettable as Aman is getting too friendly with Srinivas. Now that she has seen her

father, she thinks they can leave now. She asks
Akash to pass on the message to Aman.

"Mummy, shall we leave now?" Akash checks
with Aman.

"Who is mummy?" Srinivas checks.

"That's my nickname, sir. We will take a leave,
sir. Thank you for cooperating with the painting,"
Aman says in a hurry.

"Leave! Are you mad? You are coming home.
Have breakfast and lunch with us. What will
Arvinder sir tell me if I let you go this way?"

"Mummy," Ayush calls out before Aman
responds to the question. Aman looks at them. All
three boys and the girl are staring at Aman from a
distance.

"Excuse me, sir," he says and goes back to his
friends.

"What happened?" he asks Ayush.

"Hey, she saw her father. We are done with the
mission. Let's leave now. No need to visit their
house," Ayush anxiously speaks.

Aman looks at Padma suddenly. Coming so far
and not being able to see the mother is not a good
feeling. It's quite evident from Padma's expression.

"Earlier, I thought we shouldn't step into their
house, but now, I am adamant that we are doing it.
At least, Padma and I are doing it. If you want to
come with us, come. Otherwise, you can leave from

here. I won't mind at all," Aman says and comes
back to Srinivas before the friends respond.

"What happened? What are your friends saying?"
Srinivas checks.

"Nothing, sir. They think we should leave now for
Hyderabad and to Delhi from there. But because
you are insisting on visiting your house, I don't
think I should disobey you. Papa will not like it if
he comes to know about it," Aman says in a
nervous tone.

"Exactly! Come. Boys follow us!" Srinivas says
loudly looking at Aman's friends.

As Aman walks with Srinivas, the three boys and
the girl in a boy's attire don't move.

"But mummy has changed the plan," complains
Ayush.

"If you don't change anything, nothing will
change. I have read somewhere," Akash says and
walks towards Aman.

"The only thing that remains constant is change. I
have read somewhere," says Ghalib and follows
Akash.

Before Ayush responds to Ghalib, Padma follows
Ghalib. And why shouldn't she? Aman is doing this
for her. He is putting his life in danger to give her
some happiness.

Ayush stands there like a statue for five seconds
and then follows the rest of the group. Aman
expected this to happen. Nobody would let him fall

into a trap alone. The driver was instructed to follow them wherever they go. So, he follows the group.

Appa Rao doesn't like this. How could Srinivas impress the artists? He wishes he talked to the boys in a friendly manner initially. However, now the fish has slipped out of his hands. He should be careful next time onwards. Letting an enemy score at any front is not a good idea.

They all enter the house. Padma is almost into tears. Nobody in the group will understand the feeling of entering your house after four months. She starts shivering. The boys try to hide her behind them, so nobody recognizes her.

"Geeta, I have got some guests. Come and meet them," Srinivas screams as soon as he enters the house.

The house has a good open space at the entrance. They have partly converted it into a garden.

Geeta comes from the kitchen.

"I am sorry I am not able to recognize them," she says.

"No, no. You don't know them. This guy is Mr. Kirad's son. The others are his friends. They have come here from Delhi to capture our paddy fields in the canvases. In this entire country, they have chosen our fields. What a coincidence!"

"Please come inside. We will have breakfast. You all must have been hungry," says Geeta and escorts the children to a room inside the house.

Geeta doesn't look the way she used to look four months back. Her eyes are swollen. She has turned pale. Her voice is hoarse. It's quite evident that she hasn't taken her daughter's eloping lightly. It has taken a toll on her body.

As soon as Geeta leaves the room, the boys hear the sound of sobbing. It has to be Padma. Aman approaches her.

"Hey, what happened? You got to see your mother. Now, why are you crying? Aren't you happy?" he asks.

Padma is not in a condition to answer this question. She just wipes her tears and takes a deep breath. She has to be strong and get her composure back.

Geeta comes back with a plateful of *idlis* and a bowl full of *chutney*. Laxman's wife enters the room with five plates.

"She is Shanti, my daughter-in-law," Geeta introduces her to everyone.

Padma moves up her eyeballs to take a glance at her sister-in-law while still looking down.

Shanti smiles at Padma as they make eye contact. Padma doesn't smile back. She suddenly looks down to hide her face.

The boys' primary fear disappears now. Padma is unrecognizable by her own family members. This is, kind of, getting exciting for the boys. However, for the girl in a boy's attire, it's a once-in-a-lifetime experience. She is going through myriad emotions, all at the same time. The boys are aware of her situation but cannot help much.

"Wow! It's exactly the same taste," Ayush expresses as soon as he takes a bite of *idli*.

"Do you need anything, son?" Geeta enters the room when she hears Ayush's sudden outburst.

Ayush realizes his mistake. He meant the *idlis* Padma used to make in Delhi had the same taste. But revealing that here is suicidal.

"No, aunty. We are good. The *idlis* are very tasty," Akash covers up.

"Oh, okay! This is the specialty of Srikakulam, son. I am in the kitchen. Don't hesitate to call me in case you need anything," Geeta says and leaves the room.

"Ayush, be careful," Akash scolds Ayush as everyone looks at both of them.

"I am… I am sorry. I know it was a huge mistake," Ayush apologizes quickly. "I will be more careful," he adds and looks like has decided to keep his mouth shut.

They complete their breakfast and settle in the guest room. Shanti enters and takes the plates with her.

"Please don't bother," she says when Padma tries to help Shanti pick the plates.

As the group comes back to the open area, Padma finds Laxman standing there. For a moment, she gets shocked, fearing he may recognize her.

Laxman seems to have got the update about the guests from his parents.

"So, you people are artists? Can you draw a picture of mine?" he asks.

"Laxman! They are our guests. We shouldn't bother them with requests," Srinivas advises his son. Laxman gets a little upset.

"No worries, sir. We can do that but not now. We will have to leave now. If you can share a family picture with us, we can create the painting after reaching Delhi and send it to you with the next consignment papa sends you. Will that work?" Aman proposes.

"Yes, that works if you don't mind," says Laxman and goes inside to get a family picture. It's the same picture in the guest room that Padma kept looking at while having breakfast.

Laxman hands over the picture to Aman. He passes it on to Akash. He passes it on to Ghalib. He passes it on to Ayush. He passes it on to Padma. She holds it tight to her chest.

"Sir, we will take a leave now. Thank you for the great hospitality," says Aman.

"I thought you would wait till lunch. It would have been fun," Srinivas expresses his desire.

"No, sir. We will have to leave now," Aman resists and starts moving towards the main gate.

All this while, Padma keeps looking at her mother. And Geeta keeps staring at the boy in the corner. Padma looks away intermittently, and Geeta keeps staring at the boy with a mustache suspiciously.

"I forgot my bag in the guest room. I am going to bring it," Padma whispers in Ayush's ears, hands him the photo frame, and heads to the room where they had breakfast.

''Where is she going?'' Aman asks Ayush on seeing Padma going inside the house.

''But she was not carrying a bag! Her bag is in the car!'' Aman states.

All the boys are stunned to learn about the new development. They are trying to guess what might have happened.

Geeta has already followed Padma. Has she smelled anything fishy? That's the question in everyone's mind.

Geeta enters the room but doesn't find the boy inside the room. Strange! Where did he go?

Bam! The door is shut behind Geeta. She turns around to see the boy standing near the door, crying.

Geeta recognizes these eyes. Her second child had the same eyes when she was born. Geeta recognizes the lips. They are the same that sucked her nipples for months. The others in the family say that that girl has died for them, but how can a mother say the same? Won't it be considered ungrateful to the almighty? She hasn't yet forgotten the pain of delivering the child. It's still fresh in her mind.

Geeta moves towards the boy slowly, still doubtful of her instincts.

"Amma!" says Padma.

Confirmed! Geeta runs to her daughter and hugs her tight.

"I am sorry, amma. I made a mistake," Padma says while sobbing in her mother's arms.

"Padma!" Geeta utters. "What are you doing now? What is this avatar? Who are these boys?" she asks every question that comes to her mind.

Padma doesn't have time to answer these questions. She picks a pen from the windowsill and quickly writes her number on a piece of paper.

"I don't know when it is safe to call you. So, you give me a call when nobody is around. Amma, I am fine. So please don't fall sick, getting worried about me," says Padma and opens the door.

She joins back the boys who have engaged the family well in their talks, so nobody goes to the guest room.

The boys and Padma leave the house as swiftly as possible. As the vehicle moves, Padma is lost in her thoughts.

"Padma, all good?" Aman asks.

"Yes," Padma says as she wipes her tears. "Can we go to the police station?" she adds.

Everyone in the vehicle leans forward as the driver applies sudden brakes.

"Speed breaker, sir!" he says as the boys look at him angrily. However, that emotion doesn't last long as their focus shifts to Padma. Everyone looks at her in extreme shock. Now, what is this? Why does this girl want to go to the police station? All the men start wondering.

"Should I take a U-turn?" checks the driver. He is going to be paid per kilometer.

"Wait!" says Aman. "Why do you want to go there, Padma?" he checks with her.

"I want to appear before the police and let them know that Venky didn't kidnap me, so they can close the case against him," says Padma.

"Are you sure? Do you want to forgive him?"

"Maybe not. But he definitely didn't kidnap me. That's not true. We eloped together. He is my culprit, not of my parents," Padma states.

All the boys get into a thinking mode.

"Sounds fair. Take a U-turn," says Aman after taking a deep breath.

They reach the police station within a few
minutes. Srikakulam is not a huge city. One can
take a round of the city within half an hour in a car.
Padma approaches the inspector. She knows him.
"Sir, I want to talk to you about the case related to
Venkat Rao," she tells the inspector.
The inspector smells something fishy. The boy is
talking in a very thin voice, almost close to that of a
girl. But he doesn't think for a minute that it can be
a girl. The attire is very convincing.
"Venkat Rao, who eloped with a girl? The girl's
father has filed an FIR saying the boy kidnapped his
daughter. Are you talking about that case?"
"Yes, sir. You are right. The boy didn't kidnap the
girl. They eloped with each other. And the boy
shouldn't be blamed solely for the act," says Padma.
The inspector looks at Padma once again from top
to bottom. Padma becomes a little uncomfortable.
The inspector is staring at a boy, but she knows she
is a girl.
"How can you say this with so much confidence?
Who are you and who are all the other boys?"
"They are my friends, and I am Padma."
"What?!" The inspector is shocked.
"Sir, can I use the washroom?" asks Padma.
"Yes, it's there," the inspector points at the men's
washroom.
Padma looks in the direction the inspector
indicated and finds the ladies' washroom next to

that of the men. She quickly grabs the bag and enters the ladies' washroom.

"Hey!" calls the inspector, but it falls on deaf ears.

He is now angry. What the hell is going on! A man with a mustache enters the police station with his four friends and claims he is a woman, that too, a woman the inspector knows in person. Is this some kind of a joke? On top of that, the man uses the ladies' washroom.

"Who are you all?" The inspector screams at the top of his voice. Everyone in the police station—the staff and the visitors—looks at him. He rarely loses his cool. But how can he tolerate when a bunch of young people make fun of the police?! There is a limit to everything.

The boys are indifferent. They don't seem to be scared of the inspector. They know it will take only a couple of minutes for the inspector to realize the truth.

Since Ayush looks a little nervous, the inspector gets his prey. He grabs Ayush by his collar and asks, "Tell me. What are you all up to?"

The door of the ladies' washroom opens at this point, and it gives Ayush and the rest of the boys a sigh of relief. Ayush, still in the claws of the inspector, points at the washroom where Padma is standing in a girl's attire. Shocked, as he looks at Padma, the inspector releases Ayush from his mighty hold. The artist falls on the table, relieved.

Padma walks towards the inspector as he keeps staring at her.

"Sir, Venkat and I had eloped to Delhi. We wanted to get married. I wanted to let you know that he didn't kidnap me. I went with him willingly," she speaks in one breath.

"Padma, where have you been for so many months? Why didn't you come back when Venkat came back?" the inspector checks.

"For Venkat, it was easy, sir. His family accepted him, mine won't. Apart from that, Venkat didn't inform me when he came back. In a way, he betrayed me. If both of us decided to elope, the decision to come back should have been made by both of us. He solely chose his way back, leaving me estranged in the unknown city."

"And you still came to give the statement in favor of him?"

"Yes, sir. Because he should be punished for what he has done and not for what he hasn't done. I am here to tell you that he hasn't kidnapped me."

The inspector takes his seat as it seems he is out of shock. He has understood the entire matter now. Contrary to the popular belief in the town, the inspector is really proud of Padma. He has come across many cases like this in his career. But none of them has taken a similar turn. It needs a brave girl like Padma to make this happen. Forgiveness is not an easy trait. It takes a lot to embrace it.

As the inspector chats with the boys, he orders one of his juniors to do the paperwork. In a few minutes, Padma signs the document that has her statement and provides her phone number so the police can reach out to her in case of a requirement. Afterward, they leave the police station and the town within no time.

Chapter 9: The Friendship

"How was your trip?" Suman checks with Padma in the kitchen while they are preparing breakfast on the following Sunday.

"It was good, aunty. I didn't expect so many things would happen. I could meet my mother! Isn't that the best thing?" Padma sounds enthusiastic to describe her experience.

"Yes, Aman told me about that. But you took a huge risk. What if they recognized you?"

"I saw amma keep staring at me. I was quite sure she caught me. So, I went inside. Otherwise, she would have called me out in front of everyone, I had feared."

"Ah! This is a mother-daughter thing. A beautiful, divine bond. You have a great rapport with your mother, don't you?"

"Yes, I am very close to amma. We have always been each other's confidantes. Amma has always treated me like a friend. She has given me all the love and brought me up with extreme care. When I eloped with Venkat, it was the only thing that ate me up inside," she said.

"What?"

"I should have told her before eloping. Maybe she would have supported me and guided me better. By eloping without her knowledge, I took a friend away from her. I am her culprit," Padma says and sighs.

"What is cooking?" Aman asks as he enters the kitchen.

Padma is afraid Aman heard their conversation. She smiles at Aman quickly, so he doesn't guess it was a serious topic. Lately, she has found Aman concerned about her.

"No, nothing!" Padma answers nervously.

"Why are you getting nervous? I am literally asking what you people are preparing for breakfast," Aman explains his question to Padma.

"*Idli*! Are you hungry already?" Suman asks.

"No wonder. What can I expect when Padma is here in the kitchen?" Aman taunts.

"Why? Don't you like *idlis*?" Padma counters.

"Of course, I like them. Previously, I thought they were the best *idlis* in the world. But after I had them at your home in Srikakulam, I realized yours are a close second," the boy teases the girl.

"I know. I learned it from amma. I can't beat the teacher," the girl accepts defeat.

"Now, that sounds like a statement from a loser," says the boy. "Mummy, yes, I am hungry. The boys will reach any time. So, can you please send loads of the world's second-best *idlis* to my room?" He tells Suman and goes to his room. By 'send', Aman meant Padma should go to his room with the *idlis,* so she can contribute to the fun discussion they are going to have.

Suman enjoyed the conversation between the boy and the girl. It was healthy and entertaining. She was smiling throughout the conversation.

"You got nervous when Aman came here. What happened?" She checks with Padma as soon as Aman leaves the kitchen.

"Nothing, aunty. On my way back from Srikakulam, I promised him that I would always try to be happy. We were talking about a serious topic, and I was looking sad," Padma explains her situation.

"Oh, my God! You care about him so much!" Suman teaser the girl.

"I have to, aunty. He has saved my life," Padma says with a little hesitation.

Suman observes the awkwardness. "Okay, let's change the topic," she says quickly.

The women discuss various topics for the whole time they spend in the kitchen.

The boys gather in Aman's room in some time. Padma leaves the kitchen with a plateful of *idlis* for the boys.

Suman's eyes follow the girl till she disappears from her sight. Two tear drops fall from her eyes suddenly, enough to make her realize she is getting too attached with the girl. She takes a deep breath, gets her composure back, and serves some *idlis* on a plate for Mogambo.

As soon as Suman enters the bedroom where her husband will have the *idlis*, a roar of laughter comes from Aman's room.

"Looks like the boys are having good fun," Arvinder says after hearing the laughter.

"Yes, even the girl," says Suman with a smile.

"She is as good as the *idlis* she makes," Arvinder comments.

"What? As good as *idlis*? What do you mean?" Suman curiously asks. *"What kind of analogy is it?"* she thinks.

Arvinder never talks indirectly. He is straightforward and a man of few words. Therefore, his sudden change in mood surprises his wife.

"I meant, her nature is as soft as the *idlis* and her approach is as consistent as they are," he explains.

Those are the wisest words Suman has ever heard from her husband.

"Are you drunk?" she tries to confirm.

"No, ma'am. I am happy," he replies instantly.

"That's good. But any specific reason?" Suman asks curiously.

"Padma has taken care of all the work. I don't even need to go to the warehouse. She manages everything so brilliantly," Arvinder explains.

Suman smiles. Padma has impressed Mogambo with her work. She knew the girl had the capability. But this is exceeding her own expectations.

"Tell me something, Suman. Why did Aman go to Srikakulam?" Arvinder asks in a concerned tone.

"That's an interesting story. I didn't get a chance to tell you about it. How did you come to know about that?" Suman tries to sound innocent.

"A customer of mine found them. He took the five boys to his house as well. He described the entire incident to me. It was so embarrassing for me," Arvinder reveals.

"Why was it embarrassing?" Suman checks.

"Isn't it embarrassing to get to know about the whereabouts of our son from others?" Arvinder raises his voice. A roar of laughter comes from Aman's room again.

"I knew about it. You don't talk to us. Now, whose fault is that?" Suman complains as Arvinder pays attention to the laughter coming from his son's room.

"Ok, my fault. Leave it. Tell me something. I see Aman has three artist friends. My customer in Srikakulam said there were five boys. Who is the fifth one?"

"I also heard about it. Maybe someone they met in Hyderabad. I will check with Aman. Is it a big deal?"

"No, no. Just checking."

"Okay. You have your breakfast. I will go and check if the children have had breakfast," Suman leaves the bedroom.

Another roar of laughter comes from Aman's room as Suman walks in that direction. As she enters the room, she finds Padma standing in front of the boys and telling them some jokes.

Padma who was on a roll till now goes mum when she finds Aman's mother in the room. Everyone turns around. All the boys get disappointed to see Suman, particularly Ayush.

"What happened? Were you telling some jokes? Please continue. I would also like to listen to them," Suman tries to make Padma comfortable.

No matter how cool or friendly you become, the generation gap plays its brutal role.

Padma takes a seat quickly, and it seems she has decided not to get up till Suman is in the room.

"Oh, aunty! It was all going well till you entered the room," Ayush says disappointedly.

"*Kid! You are having fun at my house. You better watch your tongue,*" Suman so wants to say this to her son's stupid friend, but she somehow controls her anger.

"Oh, okay. I am stepping out. You people have fun then," she says and leaves the room.

Suddenly, Ayush feels someone hit him on the back of his head.

"Ouch," Ayush, who was waiting for Padma to continue her act, utters.

It is obvious that Akash is the culprit. Ayush finds Akash angry when he turns around.

"And, you had to open your mouth!" Akash shouted at his dumb friend.

Nobody knows how to handle the situation. Everyone looks at Aman with hope, but he seems to be not interested in making up for his friend's stupid act.

Who else? They wonder and look at each other.

"I will go and talk to her," Padma says as she gets up.

It is as if she has taken a huge load off everyone's shoulders. They have a sigh of relief. Aman is the only indifferent person in the room. He gets up and starts looking for some books on the shelf.

At the moment, Padma is everyone's hero. She silently leaves the room and goes to talk to or maybe apologize to Suman.

Fifteen minutes pass. Padma doesn't come back. Half an hour pass. She doesn't come back.

What must have happened? Should someone go and check? Nobody knows. Aman is still indifferent.

Ghalib thinks it's Aman's mother. If Aman doesn't care, why should he?

Akash, on the other hand, is very upset. One wrong statement from one person in the group spoiled everyone's mood. And, Ayush, of course, feels guilty about speaking his mind.

Akash finally decides to find out Padma's whereabouts and if she was able to pacify Suman. He is ready to apologize on behalf of Ayush and everyone for that matter.

Hesitantly, he moves towards the kitchen. Visiting rooms with doors in the house is not a good idea. The kitchen and dining room are the only open places he can visit.

No, they are not there in the kitchen. They must be there in the dining room. No, he doesn't find them there either. Where else can they be? He doesn't have access to any other room in the house. He better stops his investigation now.

True men turn gentlemen in the presence of women. This house, at the moment, has two women. Conscious of his limits, Akash goes back to Aman's room without searching further.

"Mummy, I couldn't find Padma and aunty in the house. Can you please go and check?" Akash requests Aman, but it sounds like a command. He has been irritated with Aman for his inactivity. Aman cannot just sit quiet and leave it to his friends to handle such a situation particularly when he is more capable than anyone else to resolve the issue.

Aman quickly keeps the book he is reading aside and gets up.

"Come," he says and steps out of the room. Akash follows him.

Aman directly goes to the guest room. The door is partially closed. Aman opens it without knocking and looking back at Akash, says, "Here they are. Now, can I go back and read my book?"

Akash doesn't get the time to respond to Aman, who is already gone. His mouth is still open.

Inside the room, Padma is doing to Suman what she was doing in front of the boys—describing funny incidents that happened on their journey. Suman is laughing uncontrollably.

Akash enters the guest room as the ladies look at him. He takes a seat and continues listening to the stories. He doesn't think he needs to apologize to Suman. She is more than happy without it.

Aman goes back to his room and starts reading again. Ghalib and Ayush look at him with the hope of an answer. Aman ignores them.

The ones who take responsibility are the ones who get the fruits of success first. Ghalib and Ayush have been passive in their approach to the situation. As expected, Ghalib gets up to find out where Akash is. He doesn't return for a long time. It leaves Ayush with no options. He finally gets up. After checking everywhere, he opens the door of the guest room and hears a burst of loud laughter immediately. He slowly enters the room as everyone looks at him.

After the last incident, Padma was describing is over, Suman asks everyone, "So, what is the moral of the story?"

There was no moral in what Padma had described. They were just anecdotes. Hence, everyone wonders what Suman means.

Suddenly, it looks like Akash gets it. "The moral of the story is—Never mess with the tiger in its den," says Akash with a smile.

"And can you mess with it anywhere else?" Suman asks Akash in a stern voice. "Anyone else?"

Akash is a little embarrassed by his answer. Ghalib, Padma, and Ayush are still bewildered.

As nobody answers, Suman says, "The moral of the story is—If you are not allowed to live in a kingdom, build your own kingdom."

Everyone gets the point now. Suman has demonstrated a behavior without preaching it to the children.

The three boys leave the house in the afternoon. Padma will leave after dinner.

Aman steps out of the house in the evening, hence it is only the ladies on evening tea on the balcony.

"Aunty, we were talking about something in the morning when the boys came in," Padma tries to recollect and remind Suman as they relish the tea with snacks.

"Hmm…" Suman tries to recollect.

"Yes, we were talking about amma!" Padma recalls.

"Yes, I was saying mother-daughter is a beautiful divine bond," Suman starts from the point they had left it.

"So, aunty, did you never wish to have a daughter?" Padma checks.

All of a sudden, Suman withdraws her smile. Her mood changes.

"Aunty! I was asking if you never wished to have a daughter," Padma makes sure her question is heard.

"Yes, I wished so, and I had one too," Suman says. She never appeared in this mood in front of Padma till now. She is sad. It's been a long time since she talked about it to someone.

"What?! Where is she? Did she elope with someone?" Padma asks innocently.

"Aman was 4 when I gave birth to her. She was 4 when we lost her," Suman doesn't look at Padma when she speaks. She is melancholic. She is in distress.

Padma doesn't know how to manage the situation. She is too young for that. She wishes she hadn't started this conversation. But it is too late now. The arrow has left the bow.

"I am sorry, aunty," Padma reacts uncomfortably.

"No, no. That's okay. It's been a long time. I have moved on long back," Suman expresses. "You know what? You haven't seen me sad in this house, have you? I am always happy, aren't I?" she checks.

"Yes, aunty. I always found you in a jovial mood. That's true," Padma agrees.

"You know Mogambo, how he is. I can't talk to him about anything. He is not a person with whom I can share my feelings. Aman is a boy. I won't be able to open up to him as well. So, I keep my feelings to myself," Suman opens up.

"You don't have any friends, aunty?" Padma checks.

"I used to have in Amrutsar. I was in touch with them for a few years after my marriage. Now, they are all busy with their own lives. I am not in touch with them."

Padma understands the pains of living in a big city. People are locked in apartments, busy earning money. They are not interested in human relationships. If there is anything, it is the bond of convenience. Suman is lonely in this extremely crowded city.

"Aunty, I am a couple of years younger than Aman. Can't you treat me like your daughter?" Padma says hesitantly, with all good intent. These are difficult conversations.

"No!" Suman says instantly.

Padma gets nervous. Why did she have to propose that? She has been provided with refuge in this house, trusted with the business, and treated so well.

And she now dares be a part of the family, taking such an important position!

Suman can see how uncomfortable Padma is.

"You can't be my daughter, Padma. I don't have that privilege in my life. I am doomed. I have lost one, and I don't want to put you in that position and lose you. You are my friend, my confidante, not my daughter," she says.

Padma is overwhelmed by Suman's words. It's intense. She reacts thoughtfully. Now, Suman is a little embarrassed. Should she have proposed being a friend of a girl of her son's age? She can be friendly but calling her a friend can be a little too much.

"Are you thinking about how I can be your friend?" Suman asks hesitantly. "Is it because of the age gap?"

"No, no, aunty. I am not thinking about that. I am feeling overwhelmed. It's an honor to be your friend. But do you think I am worthy of it?"

"We have been friends, Padma. We just didn't talk about it ever. Look back at how we spent time together. Don't you agree with me?"

Padma takes a sip of the tea as she thinks. Yes, Suman is right. They have always been friends. In fact, Padma is more comfortable with Suman than with her friends in Srikakulam.

"Are you as comfortable with me as you used to be with your friends in Amritsar?" Padma checks.

"Yes! In fact, more than that."

Padma thinks of something and smiles.

"What happened?" Suman checks as she takes a sip of tea.

"No, I was thinking…" Padma hesitates to complete the sentence.

"Yes, what were you thinking?" Suman checks.

"I was thinking we are talking like we are in a relationship."

"Yes, we are friends, right?"

"Not that way. Like…" she pauses.

"Like?"

"Like a love relationship," she doesn't look at Suman, feels shy.

"Oh, yeah!" Suman gets what Padma tries to indicate. "Relationships sometimes overlap each other; don't you think so?" she asks.

"Meaning?" Padma checks.

"Relationships are about how much you can share with a person. We share certain things with our parents, siblings, female friends, male friends, and spouses. Similarly, we hide certain things from each of them. The extent to which we share or hide determines our relationship," Suman describes and then becomes doubtful if a 22-year-old girl will understand the intensity of the subject.

"That's such a nice way to put it, aunty," Padma reacts. "And you say they overlap because what you share with one person can be shared with another too," she adds.

"Wow! See how much we are aligned. I didn't have to explain in detail. You got it instantly," Suman is surprised.

"I find this thought very interesting. You put it so beautifully, aunty," Padma expresses.

"It's not my thought, originally. I read it in a book called 'The Wedding Picture'. But I agree with the thought and endorse it now," says Suman. "And Padma, now that we are friends, can you stop calling me 'aunty'?" Suman asks.

Padma is not sure what else to address Suman as.

"What else can I call you then?"

"Suman! That's my name," Suman says instantly. That will be difficult for me.

"Why? Friends call each other by their first name, don't they?"

"Yes. But they do that from the very first day," Padma argues.

"Okay. Let me be fair with you. I have been addressing you as Padma. I will also change it. Let me choose another name for you," Suman says and starts thinking of a new name.

Padma finds it funny. She is excited to know what name Suman is going to come up with.

"Padma is one of the names of a goddess. So, I will call you 'Devi'. Is that fine, Devi?" says Suman.

Padma is amazed. It's a good name. She likes it.

"Yes," she says as she nods her head. She gets up, approaches Suman, hugs her tight, and says, "Yes, Suman. That works."

They both have tears in their eyes. They needed each other badly. They didn't have anyone to open up to. It's important to open up to someone. The emotional baggage needs to be taken off. One cannot lift the load all the time. Finally, the ladies find each other to take the load off each other's hearts.

Chapter 10: The Nine Moods

"Mummy! Good news!" Aman comes running to Suman, screaming. It's a Saturday evening. Suman is sitting alone on the balcony, having tea. She was in a different mood till her son disturbed her chain of thoughts.

"What happened?" Suman excitedly checks as she puts the cup on the table.

"I got a call from the Hyderabad Art Society. My painting is going to be part of an art museum they are creating!" Aman speaks in one breath.

He is as happy as a poor person feels when they win millions in a lottery. For him, art is everything. He finds happiness there. He finds solace, satisfaction, and refuge there. He expresses his emotions through his art. He feels free when he paints.

Suman too feels exhilarated. This is big news. This is a dream come true for an artist, even though it's not the ultimate dream. But Aman and Suman arc people who try to see the future to the horizon.

Once they reach there, they look beyond that. They will have to weave new dreams now and set new goals. Seeing this dream getting fulfilled gives them more confidence to weave new ones. However, this was not even there on their cards. Aman went to Hyderabad with no expectations. It was just a casual visit. He didn't expect to get success this way.

"Wait! I will call Padma and tell her," Suman thinks of her new friend first with whom she wants to share the news.

"No, no. Don't call her. We will surprise her when she comes here tomorrow. I want to see her expression when she gets the news," Aman proposes.

Suman is happy to know how her son treats her friend. "Okay, we will do it that way," she agrees.

"However, mummy…" it seems Aman has more news.

"What happened? Tell me," Suman insists.

"That was only one painting. They need eight more," says Aman.

"So what? You can create them, right?" Suman asks.

"It's not easy. They have given me a theme and you very well know I don't follow themes."

"That can't be a forever attitude. Shouldn't be difficult for you. What's the theme?" Suman asks.

"Nine moods," Aman reveals.

"What's that?"

"They are love, humor, compassion, anger, courage, fear, disgust, wonder, and peace."

"The painting that I displayed in the exhibition this time represented one of these nine moods, which is 'Courage'."

"Oh! So, you need eight more?"

"That's not what I need. That's what they want."

"So, you have to make them, right?"

"No, I will tell them I don't work that way. I am happy that they considered my painting to be a part of it. I won't be able to collaborate with them further," Aman bluntly says.

"Are you mad?"

"No, mummy. But you know I don't have that skill," Aman argues.

"Dear, before you became an artist, you didn't know you had the skills to become an artist. You will have to find your way out to solve this problem. Not everyone gets such opportunities. Your friends didn't get lucky either. You are the chosen one. You will have to make the best out of it," Suman tries to persuade her adamant son.

"You are right, mummy. But it's so difficult for me. I need to get involved to paint something. These people want me to paint the same character in nine moods. Do you think that's possible?" Aman reveals his concerns.

"Yes, that's definitely possible. Not for everyone. But for Aman Kirad, it's possible," Suman caresses

Aman's shoulder. Love may work where logic cannot. "Let me bring some tea for you," she says and goes to the kitchen.

"You didn't have any reference when you created that painting, did you?" Suman asks while walking back with a cup of tea for Aman. "Padma was not here when you painted, was she?" she adds to her question.

Aman just looks at Suman as she tries to motivate him. He is still in doubt about his own skills. Suman gauges that.

"Son, if you restrict yourself so much, then you will remain what you are now. Get out of your comfort zone. Create what you haven't created. Do what you haven't done yet. Don't kill it before it is born. Your aim shouldn't be to create one masterpiece but to get into the habit of keeping creating them," Suman persuades Aman as he starts sipping tea from the cup.

"How is the tea, dear?" she checks casually.

"It's good," Aman says as he takes another sip.

"See, you normally don't like to have tea. But you are having it now and liking it. Likewise, give it a try, dear."

Aman is almost sold to his mother's arguments. He starts considering her ideas.

"She is right. I was not willing to go to the art classes. She is the one who recognized my skill in me and lure me to go to the classes. I was not able

to see what she could. Maybe history is repeating itself. If I don't reinvent myself, I will remain the same. And the same is boring, unsatisfactory; stagnancy has a foul smell," he thinks.

Suman gauges Aman is convinced.

"Why don't you spend more time with Padma? Who knows? You may be able to see the nine moods in her for your reference," she says as soon as Aman comes back from his thoughts.

"That will be so selfish of me, mummy."

"I think it's okay. We will apologize to her later. Maybe when she comes to know about our purpose and sees the output, she will forgive us and appreciate our intent," Suman assures. "But we can't let her know the purpose now, otherwise she won't execute the moods naturally," she adds.

"Okay, I will leave that to you, mummy. I promise I will do my best with the paintings," Aman says as he takes the last sip of tea from the cup.

∷∷∷∷

"Hello!" Padma says as she arrives in the evening after work. Suman asked her to come home to discuss something.

"Hey! You came directly from the store. Go freshen up! We will have tea," Suman advises.

"Okay," Padma says and goes inside the washroom.

Suman serves the tea and snacks on a tray and goes to the gallery where she plans to have a discussion with Padma.

"So, what is that important thing you want to discuss? Is Mogambo having an affair?" Padma jokes as soon as she comes to the gallery.

"I wish he had one," Suman says with a disappointed face. "They say an affair repairs a marriage, don't they?" They both laugh after Padma gives a shocked look and Suman winks at her.

"Tell me, no? What happened?" Padma asks impatiently.

"Sit and have tea first. I am not going to elope with anyone," Suman advises.

Padma has no other choice than to suppress her curiosity for some time.

"I need a favor from you," says Suman after taking a sip of tea.

"Yes, tell me," It seems Padma has already agreed to help her friend out.

"It's about Aman, Devi," Suman says and takes another sip of tea.

Padma is not liking this suspense build-up. "Yes, what is it?" she asks.

"Aman has got an offer from the Hyderabad Art Society. He needs to create more paintings for them."

"Oh, wow! That's great news, isn't it?" Some tea from Padma's cup spill over and fall on her fingers and ground as she moves her hand swiftly out of excitement.

"But there is a problem," Suman says as Padma wipes her fingers with her handkerchief.

"What's that?"

"You know how Aman is. He locks himself in the room and doesn't venture out. He is an introvert, just like his father. But for art, you need to get inspiration from the world. You need to observe what's there outside."

Padma keeps listening thoughtfully. She doesn't understand how she will be able to help here.

"He finds it difficult to visualize what he needs to paint. That's why he doesn't want to take the deal," Suman adds.

"What! That is such an excellent opportunity. He shouldn't let go of it. It is stupidity. He is such a good artist. This opportunity will take him one step ahead in his career," Padma speaks up.

"Exactly! But he is in no mood to listen to me. Art gives him pleasure and happiness. For it to be his profession, he has to consider it more than just a way of expressing himself. He has to make his art relate to others, and touch others' hearts. For that to happen, he needs to take new challenges."

"Okay! Now, please tell me what I can do here," Padma impatiently asks. She has made up her mind to do anything that Suman proposes to her.

"It might not excite you…" Suman tries to pitch her idea properly.

"Leave that to me. Just tell me what I can do," Padma is running out of patience by the second.

"Aman needs to paint nine different moods of a human being. I think he has to step out and look around for inspiration," Suman moves one step ahead in her pitch.

"What can I do here?" Padma starts getting irritated.

"Okay! Can you come here after the office and take him out with you? Go to parks, restaurants, movies, anywhere you want to. Just take him out of his room," Suman attempts to end the suspense.

"Do you think that will help? He can do that with his artist friends as well," Padma asks. "I mean I am just asking," she tries to defend her idea.

"I don't think so. He needs to look beyond art. He needs to look at life the way it is. Observe. I think you are the only one at this moment who can do this. Now, tell me if you can do this or not," Suman sounds a little intimidating.

It sounds like her friendship with Suman is at stake now. Suman has never asked her for any favor. This is the first time she is asking for something. Padma cannot refuse it. And it's not the question of whether she wants or not, it's about whether she is capable or not.

"Do you think he would like to go out with me?"
Padma asks the last question with an innocent face.
"I am sure he will love to do that. If not, I will
convince him. Thanks for helping me, Devi. I
promise I will return this favor sometime."
"Now, this is wrong. You cannot mention the
words like 'favor', 'thank you' and all in
conversations," Padma complains cutely.
"Okay, dear. I am sorry," Suman keeps the teacup
on the table and holds both her ears to apologize.
She looks even cuter.
But for some reason, Padma looks at her angrily.
"I can say 'sorry', right? Or, that word is banned
too?" Suman checks.
Padma starts laughing and Suman joins her too.
They both look beautiful this way. They should
laugh quite often.

∴∷∴

Arvinder leaves for the store early today. There
are multiple consignments to be delivered. Padma
must have reached the store from the hostel.
"She will come today in the evening," Suman says
to Aman over breakfast.
"Did you tell her the purpose?"
"No, are you mad? I told her to go out with you so
you can see the world and take inspiration," Suman
explains.
"And she agreed?"

"Yes. Instantly."

"She will think you are observing the world. Only you and I know that you are observing her."

Aman smiles slightly on hearing this. "I feel like you are doing matchmaking here," he says.

"Everything is fair in love and art," Suman says as she smiles back at her son.

"But remember! Don't flirt with her. I don't want you to flirt with my friend," she warns him.

"What! You are taking the side of a stranger against your son!"

"Of course! I have two reasons for that. Both of us are women, and we are friends," Suman argues.

"Oh, forget it. She is not my type."

"I wish she was your type. If you had married her, she would have lived in this house. Then, she and I would have taken the case of both the men in this house."

"Mummy! What are you saying? I am done with the breakfast," says Aman and gets up to wash his hands. He pretends to be irritated with his mother.

∷∷∷

Aman and Padma walk the roads of Delhi this evening, sometimes separately and sometimes hand-in-hand. For an onlooker, they will seem like a couple in love. They are comfortable this way. For Aman, it's a common behavior as he was born and brought up in a big city. Padma took some time to adjust to the new behavior. She is like any Delhi girl now.

"Did you find any inspiration, Aman?" Padma asks as they walk through a subway.

"Not exactly!" Aman says uncomfortably.

"Ok. I think I should not ask you this question. Otherwise, you will feel the pressure, and that's not good for the purpose," says Padma after gauging the discomfort in Aman's voice.

Aman nods his head. Padma's realization is good for him. He couldn't have passed on the message to her.

:::::::::

They have spent every evening together in the last week. No breakthrough for Aman. He just holds the brush in his hand and stands in front of the canvas.

"You are painting, dear?" Suman asks him as she enters Aman's room with a cup of tea.

"No! I am trying to," Aman says with a bit of frustration.

"Please don't try then. Have tea," says Suman.

"We have only three weeks to go, mummy," Aman reminds his mother.

"I know. Don't think of the timeline. Delivering the paintings to them is not our priority but you being able to paint is. If it doesn't happen on time, it's ok. Artists take their own time. They shouldn't be put under irrational pressure."

"You are talking as if you are an artist," Aman taunts his mother unintentionally.

"I am the mother of one. And to your point, I would like to say, one who appreciates good art is no less than an artist."

"Wow! What a lovely thought!"

"Not mine. It's from the book '14 Nights and the Wedding Gift'. It's an interesting book."

"I will read it. Please give it to me once you are done," Aman says as he keeps the brush aside and takes the teacup from Suman's hand.

At that moment, Padma arrives. They are planning to visit the India Gate today.

"Did he get any breakthrough, Suman?" Padma inquires about the status as soon as she gets an opportunity.

"Not yet. But are you tired of going out with him every day?"

"Not at all. I can do it for the rest of my life."

"Aww... I can't even say 'thank you'," Suman appreciates the gesture without words.

❖❖❖❖❖

They get down at the Central Secretariat metro station. They will take a walk from here. In the last week, they have talked about every topic. They don't have any topic to discuss now. So mostly, they remain silent.

Suddenly, Padma's eyes fall on an animal on the road. It's a kitten. A nervous kitten. It is standing in the middle of the road, trying to cross the road. "Aman!" Padma utters. "Do you see that cat?" Aman looks in the direction Padma is pointing at. He sees the cat and in a couple of seconds, he sees Padma near the cat. She has rushed to rescue the cat without giving it any thought. Motorcycles, cars— nobody has time to stop. They couldn't stop to save the kitten earlier nor can they stop now for the safety of a human being. She has to dodge all the vehicles to reach back safely. Aman gets worried. However, before he takes any action, Padma and the kitten are back on the footpath.

As Padma caresses the kitten, she sees a tea stall nearby and considers giving the animal some milk to drink.

She walks to the stall and looks at Aman who, understanding her signals, asks the man in the stall for some milk immediately.

"This kitten will die like its mother, sir," the man says while pouring some milk on a paper plate.

Padma gets worried upon hearing this.

"Why? Why do you say so?" she asks.

"Its mother was crushed by a truck two days ago while she was crossing the road," he says.

Aman looks at Padma. She is sad. Caressing the kitten, she looks at Aman and says, "Can we take it home?"

Aman smiles. He also wanted to propose the same thing. He calls a taxi, and they return home from that place with the kitten.

Suman gets the honor of naming the kitten. And the name that immediately comes to her mind is 'Lucy'.

The next morning, Aman draws his first painting of the series and names it Compassion. It features Padma with Lucy.

Suman takes a look at the painting. She is in awe of it. Her son is on the right path.

"We will show it to Padma," Suman says immediately. "She will be happy to see this."

"No, mummy. If she finds this out, she will not go out with me. And if she does, she won't be herself," Aman opposes the idea.

"Oh yeah! Sorry, I forgot," Suman apologizes.

This evening, Suman wants to join Aman and Padma. They are planning to go to a restaurant to have dinner. As Padma is asked to select a restaurant of her choice, she goes for a restaurant that serves good South Indian food.

"Which mood are you looking for today?" Suman whispers in Aman's ears as they wash their hands together.

"Mummy, it's not right to talk behind your friend's back," Aman taunts. "By the way, to answer your question, it's nothing in particular. Beggars cannot be choosers," he jokes.

The three have given their order and are waiting for food when a man shouts out with joy. "Oh, my God! South Indian food is the best food in the world."

The man is sitting behind Padma, so she has to turn around to see him. Aman and Suman can see the man. Suman is quite amused by the sudden outburst of the man, but Aman gets irritated.

"Wow! This is impressive. Look at this. They made *Dosa*, then they thought of having a variety of stuffings, then they made *chutney*, then they made *sambhar*. How clever they are! They have something for everyone's taste buds," the elderly man is louder than last time.

From his attire i.e., the beard, mustache, and turban, it looks like the man is from Punjab, the home state of Suman. He is talking to his wife. The wife seems to be embarrassed about the husband's loud expressions. She looks at Suman who passes on the message "it's okay" through her eyes.

Aman's expression talks louder than words. In his mind, it goes, "*Oh gosh, these people! They don't know how to behave in public.*" Suman pushes his elbow and talks to him through her eyes, "*It's okay, Aman. Don't make them conscious.*"

Padma is enjoying the whole incident. And why
not? Someone is praising her favorite food so
loudly.

Before the food arrives on their table, the elderly
couple gets up to wash their hands. As the couple
passes them, the lady comes to Suman and
apologizes to her. Then, she caresses Padma's chin
with her left hand and says, "Very pretty girl."
Padma is about to blush when the lady looks at
Aman and continues, "What a beautiful couple!"

Suman starts smiling naughtily as the lady leaves.
It leaves Aman and Padma embarrassed. Suman
keeps smiling, recollecting the incident throughout
the dinner. It is time for Aman to talk through his
eyes, "*Mummy, stop it, please!*"

Padma plans to have a night out with the Kirads.
They reach home and start discussing the incident.

"That uncle was so loud, but you know what was
funnier? The way Aman got irritated with him. And
his wife's comment when they were leaving. Aman
almost killed them in his thoughts," Padma says,
laughing uncontrollably, holding her stomach.

Everyone goes to sleep after a while and Aman
paints. He completes one more painting of the series
and names it Humor.

Today, Aman doesn't want to go out. He is not
feeling good. The food that he had in the restaurant

yesterday did magic in his stomach. He is just idling on the balcony when Padma arrives. She gets his health update from Suman. So, it will be a light conversation, dinner, and bidding goodbye on Padma's to-do list this evening.

When Suman comes to the balcony with two cups of tea on a tray, the boy and the girl are sitting there like strangers. She doesn't like this mood at all. Her husband and son are always silent and in a thinking mood. Now, her friend is also becoming like them.

"Looks like this nature is contagious," Suman thinks. *"No, I won't let Padma look sad, lost, or thoughtful all the time,"* she tells herself.

Something strikes her mind. She keeps the tray on the table and goes inside. The tray is lying on the table like an orphan. Padma doesn't pick her cup of tea. The other cup is for Suman.

Suddenly, Padma screams. She gets scared. And who won't be? If an animal with sharp nails jumps on the chest all of a sudden, anyone would react in the same manner.

Padma, after getting her composure back, realizes what happened just now. Suman has thrown the cat on Padma to break the ice.

"Next time, I see you in this sad mood, I will throw anything that comes to my hand at you," Suman warns.

Padma is still keeping her hands close to her chest. Struggling to smile, she is complaining through her eyes, *"What the hell you have done?"*

Aman gets up and goes inside his room and locks himself.

"What happened to him?" Padma checks with Suman.

"Nothing. The men in the house are mad. He must have got an idea for a painting. He will now come out of his room only after his painting is done," Suman reveals.

When Aman comes out of the room, the scene outside has changed. Suman is done with dinner. Padma has gone back to the hostel. He sits at the dining table and requests his mother to serve dinner.

"Thanks, mummy. I have created one more painting in the nine moods series," Aman says as Suman is serving him food.

"Is it? What is the mood you covered today?" Suman asks curiously.

"Fear!"

∷∷∷

A few more days have passed, and Aman hasn't made any progress with the paintings in the series. His score is 4/9 now. When he got a call from the Hyderabad Art Society, he informed them that he needs more time to create the paintings. The art society has agreed to give him more time.

They decided to watch a movie today. Aman thought Padma would react to different scenes in the movie and he would get what he wanted.

Just before they enter the theater, a couple of girls call out Aman.

"Hey, what a surprise," Aman says.

"What are you doing here? You are not someone who watches movies," one of the girls says.

"Padma! Give me two minutes. I will come," Aman says as Padma walks into the theater.

"Okay!" Padma looks back and responds.

"Are you serious? You have come to watch a movie with her! Who is she?" says the other girl with a disgusted face.

"Why? What happened?" Aman doesn't understand what the girl meant.

"I mean you are so cool, and she looks dumb," the girl decodes her statement. She is wearing modern clothes and looks very stylish with colored hair and makeup applied.

"Sonia, this is rude. She is a nice person, and you have no right to comment about her. You haven't met her yet. How can you judge people like that?" Aman gets angry with his old friend.

"Oops! I am sorry, Aman. I have commented on your countryside girlfriend," she teases and makes funny faces. The other girl starts laughing.

"Now, this is enough. Get lost," Aman says and gets inside the theater where Padma is waiting for him.

"What happened? You look upset," Padma checks as they take their seats after the National Anthem is complete.

"Nothing," he responds. He looks even more upset now.

"You look so cute when you get angry," Padma comments.

"How can someone look cute when they get angry?" Aman sounds irritated.

"You do. But you shouldn't mind your friend's comments. She is right," she advises.

"You heard her?" he asks in a concerned tone.

"Yes. She called me 'dumb' and 'countryside'. She was loud enough for me to hear. Maybe she purposely did so."

"Are you not upset to hear that?"

"No. Even I think she is dumb. Even I am being judgmental about her. I don't know her yet. She might be a good person, who knows?"

Aman thinks to himself. "Yeah! If you don't care, it doesn't matter. I shouldn't think about her comments much."

"Jealousy makes you do many things, you know. It's not she but her jealousy was speaking. She must be thinking how this girl can watch a movie with this handsome boy. Why couldn't I?" Padma says in a funny tone.

This brings a smile to Aman's face.

"Thanks for understanding," he says as they start watching the movie.

A few minutes into the movie, Padma seems to be bored. She doesn't enjoy such movies. There isn't any item song nor is there a fight sequence. She just waits for the interval. Aman is engrossed in the movie. Sitting at the edge of his seat, he doesn't even blink.

Finally, the moment that Padma has been waiting for arrives—the interval.

"Do you like it?" Aman asks as soon as the lights are on.

Padma makes an expression that means 'no'. She looks cute when she makes such faces, at least, to Aman.

They step out of the theater during the interval and get some popcorn and cold drinks.

As Padma holds her share of snacks and walks towards the theater, Sonia crashes into her and as a result, everything Padma was holding is spread on the ground.

"I am so sorry," Sonia apologizes in a pretentious tone.

Aman comes running to the spot to avoid any clashes between the girls.

Padma had forgiven Sonia for her comments last time. She doesn't seem to be in the mood of forgiving her this time. Now that her hands are free, she gives one tight slap to Sonia. It is so tight that the receiver will go deaf for a few minutes.

"Your apparel won't display your status, but your conduct will. You don't even know me and still, you are getting jealous of me. Then, what do you have in life? Nothing, right?" Padma makes a zero using the thumb and index fingers of her right hand.

Sonia has got the shock of her life. She didn't expect such a reaction from a girl whom she considered dumb and from the countryside. She is almost into tears.

Before Sonia reacts to avenge the slap, Aman drags Padma out of the place. They leave for home without watching the rest of the movie.

"I am sorry I lost my cool. I shouldn't have slapped her," Padma apologizes as Aman drives the car.

"I am happy you did that, Padma. I wanted to do so but a boy slapping a girl wouldn't have sounded good," Aman sounds delighted.

"How do you know her?" Padma checks as she thinks Sonia doesn't deserve to be his friend.

"She was from my school. She asked me out a couple of times, but I refused," he says.

"Wow! It seems you were very popular in school," Padma comments.

"I don't think so. I was an introvert. Didn't talk to anyone. Akash was the only person I would talk to."

"But she is very pretty. Why didn't you go out with her?"

"You saw her. Does prettiness mean skin type, body structure, how well you have painted your face, or how scantily or colorfully you have covered your body? She is not my type."

"Then, what is your type?" Padma instantly asks without thinking. "I mean, if you want to tell me..." she says as she gets intimidated by Aman's look.

"No idea. But I will let you know when I come to know," he says and shifts his focus back to the road.

He drops Padma at the hostel directly and leaves for home.

Before going to bed, he creates the next painting in the series and names it Anger.

In two weeks, Aman's score is 5/9. Four more to go. Even though the art society has given him more time, he is planning to complete the pending four paintings on time. But how? He doesn't know. There is no scarcity of skills, but inspiration is all that he needs.

"Aman told me you hit her hard," Suman checks with Padma when she arrives.

"It's so embarrassing," Padma reacts shyly.

"Aman has gone out with the boys. Let's have fun today."

"Has he created any painting, Suman? Was I of any help?"

"I would say, 'yes'. Not one but multiple of them. But he doesn't want to show them to us until he completes all eight of them."

"O wow! That's great. I am so happy I could help. Can you imagine? You just need to hang out with an artist and then he creates amazing paintings. It's unbelievable, isn't it?"

"It is. And it is very unique."

Padma wants to take Suman's opinion on something. But she hesitates to ask.

"What happened? Do you want to ask something?" Suman checks with her when she gauges the hesitation.

"No. I mean…"

"Say, no? Why are you hesitating?"

Padma takes a deep breath and thinks for a few seconds. Then, she feels she needs to throw up.

"Do I look dumb?"

"Oh! You are taking that Sonia too seriously. Forget it."

"No, no. It's not about her. I also want to look modern."

Suman looks at her with a naughty smile.

"I didn't mean wearing the clothes she wore. But you know? The hair color, heels, and things like that," Padma hesitantly expresses.

"Hmm... I think you should do whatever you want to. We will go to the parlor and shopping this Sunday. Will that work?"

"Yes," Padma shyly responds.

They talk for some time and then Padma starts a new activity at Suman's insistence.

Aman comes home running.

"Mummy, did Padma come today?" he checks immediately.

Suman comes rushing from the guest room.

"Shh..." she asks Aman to keep his voice low. "What happened?"

"I am teaching her how to control her anger. She is meditating."

"Can I see her?"

"Why do you want to see her?"

"Please!"

"Okay, don't disturb her though," Suman says and goes to the kitchen to prepare dinner.

Aman enters the guest room.

15 minutes pass. During this time, Padma hasn't opened her eyes and Aman hasn't taken his eyes off Padma.

This girl was like wildfire yesterday when she was angry. Now she looks like still water.

Aman has seen many moods of Padma till now. But this mood is his favorite. Maybe, he starts falling for her for the first time now. He has never felt this way for anyone in his life. His heart starts beating faster. He feels like staring at her continuously. Suddenly Lucy enters the room and makes her signature sound "Miaow…" which breaks his chain of thoughts. Padma opens her eyes too fearing Suman may throw the kitten at her. As soon as their eyes meet, Aman gets up and exits the guest room quickly. He locks himself in his room for the rest of the evening.

Padma didn't know when Aman came into the room and what he was doing there. She doesn't pay much heed to that.

Only after Padma leaves the house does Aman comes out of his room to have dinner. The glimpse of Padma meditating runs in his mind the whole night. It's an irony that one gets disturbed on seeing the other being calm.

In the morning, Aman creates the next painting in the series and names it Peace.

꠸꠸꠸꠸꠸

A couple of days passed, and Aman was unable to make any progress. The pending paintings are for the moods of Disgust, Wonder, and Love.

As he has started falling for Padma, he feels a little uncomfortable talking to her. He fears he might hurt her in some way. He has now become possessive about her. In the morning when Padma comes home, Aman feels happy. He thinks he will get some time to spend with her. But Padma and Suman have different plans.

Padma and Suman quickly have breakfast and leave for their outing.

"Please wash your own plate today," Padma tells Aman before leaving as he is still licking his fingers sitting at the dining table.

Padma gets a brown color for her hair similar to Sonia. Her hair hasn't grown much since she had cut it short last time to look like a boy.

Suman feels she doesn't look better now but is definitely different. Nevertheless, Padma is feeling better as she did something she wanted to do.

They go shopping and buy modern clothes, sandals, bags, cosmetic stuff, etc. Then, they decide to walk back home. On the way back, Padma finds a well-shaped tree. On the branches of the tree, some beautiful birds are resting. One of the branches is within Padma's reach. She can hold it and hang from it. But that's not what she wants. She wants Suman to take her photograph with the branch and the birds. She wants to flaunt her new hair color.

Suman is getting a little irritated with Padma today. Her friend is behaving like a child. But she understands it. Padma is just 22 years old, and she is behaving her age. That's normal.

Padma takes her position under the branch as Suman tries to adjust the picture frame on her phone. The birds are still there. Padma has tried not to scare them.

Perfect frame. "Smile," Suman says and touches the Capture button with her right thumb.

At the very moment, Padma feels something has fallen on her head, something wet. She looks up, only to find that the birds have flown away after defecating on her head. The moment gets captured in the photograph. Suman laughs her heart out continuously until they reach home. Padma takes a shower immediately.

Aman has been upset with her mother today. He could have got some inspiration if he had got time to spend with Padma. *"But, no, mummy had to step out with her,"* he thinks.

At the dinner table, when Aman displays her anger toward his mother, she tries to make his mood better by showing him a funny picture. As Aman looks at the picture, Suman describes the entire incident. The narration cheers him up. But more than that, the picture inspires Aman to create the next painting in the series—Disgust.

Aman has now fallen for Padma. He is waiting for an opportunity to gauge what's in her mind. Unofficially, they are kind of dating these days. His mother, without her own knowledge, has been playing the role of a matchmaker.

When he had taken a nap before Padma arrived, he dreamt of Padma.

She was getting married. She was looking immensely beautiful as a bride. In all the pre-wedding rituals, Padma had loads of fun. She was laughing throughout. She danced too on occasions. But she waited for the ultimate moment, the moment when she would finally see her bridegroom. How would he be dressed up? How would he look at her? How would he react when he looked at her? How should she react when she looked at him? She kept thinking of all these questions.

Finally, the moment came when Padma got to see her bridegroom. However, his face was not visible completely. She was not sure who he was. She got anxious. Would it be someone I love? Would it be someone I don't know? A stranger, an acquaintance? Who would it be? She kept wondering.

Suman appeared in front of her sight. She gave her assurance that the bridegroom is someone she loves. And, when Suman moved aside, Padma could see Aman. Dressed as the bridegroom, he was looking at his best. All his artist friends were walking behind him.

A wide smile appeared on Padma's face when she saw Aman smiling at her. She was almost into tears.

She didn't know how to control her emotions. Her mother held her tight. It was as if she was telling her, "Padma, control yourself."

As they came closer, they could only see each other. The world paused for them. Aman kept staring at Padma, and she kept gazing at him with immense love. It was the love for which one would be ready to sacrifice everything.

Aman was supposed to put the garland around Padma's neck. But he was too lost to do that. Everyone tried to get him back to his senses. Neither Aman nor Padma had a sense of belonging to the world. "Aman," Suman called out loudly.

"Aman, Padma has arrived," she called out again.

The second time, the voice was loud enough to get Aman out of his dreams.

Aman is now thinking about the meaning of his dream. He is thinking of Padma too much. She has occupied her subconscious mind. His feelings for her are so deep that he has started dreaming of marrying her.

"Am I going too fast? Is it possible? I think I should express my feelings to her," Aman thinks to himself. He gets up and goes to the balcony where Padma and Suman are discussing. He doesn't want to step out today. He has already got an idea for his next painting. He rather sits there with Padma and

talks to her for hours when Suman leaves them alone.

Padma knows where this conversation is going. She is getting attracted to Aman. She is falling for him. It hasn't started now. She doesn't know when it started. But one thing that she knows is that Aman is out of her range. He can never like her. She has seen his old friends. They are too stylish, modern, and bold. A hair color, a pair of sandals, and a skirt will not make Padma look like those girls. So, she should suppress her feelings and save her friendship with the mother of her crush.

As a result, Aman finds Padma disinterested when he talks about love.

"*Maybe it's not the right time. I will tell her some other day,*" he thinks.

After Padma leaves, Aman creates the next painting of the series and names it Love.

Aman got a call from the art society today. One of their vehicles will be in Delhi tomorrow and they want to collect everything that Aman has created by now. Aman had sent the pictures of the paintings to them over a message. They loved them. It's approved instantly.

"Mummy, we will have to pack the paintings now. Their vehicle will arrive in the morning tomorrow. The driver will come and collect them,"

"Are you done with all?"

"No, only one is pending. They will collect that later."

"Which mood is pending?" Suman checks curiously.

"Wonder," he reveals.

Suman thinks about it for a minute as Aman waits for her response.

"Hey, it will be rude to send them to Hyderabad without showing them to Padma. She might not get a chance to see them again," she proposes.

"I have the pictures on my phone," he says.

"You may have them, but you know what I mean. A painting is a painting, and a picture of a painting is a picture," she argues.

Aman hesitates a bit. Suman understands his fears.

"I know what you are thinking. You still have to paint the last mood and you don't want to reveal it to her before that, right?"

"Yes," Aman agrees.

"You will have to create that without reference, Aman. Sending the paintings without showing her is rude and disregarding her favors," Suman tries to convince him.

"And, you know what? I so want to see them," she looks excited.

Aman agrees with his mother's thoughts. She makes sense.

"Let's call her then," he says.

"Let's call the three boys as well," Suman proposes.

Aman likes this idea as well.

"Mummy, I don't want you to come to my room. I want to show the paintings to everyone at once. Let me arrange them in my room."

Suman agrees with the idea. She needs to have patience too.

The plan is set. Padma agrees to leave the store now. The three boys agree to leave everything they are doing and come to see Aman's paintings.

Suman starts preparing snacks for everyone.

Within an hour, the group gathers in the guest room. Aman's room is locked from the inside. Suman has instructed everyone not to knock on his door. Aman will open it when he is ready.

Different thoughts are running through the minds of different people.

"*Let me see how good they are. Can they be better than mine?*" Ayush wants to compare Aman's paintings with his.

"*I will need to remain silent and not criticize if I don't like the paintings. Aunty will get angry otherwise,*" Ghalib warns himself.

"*I am so proud of this guy. All that I needed to do was to hang out with him and he could observe the surroundings to take inspiration for his paintings,*" Padma thinks.

"I am sure Aman has created a few masterpieces. He is definitely a better artist than me. It's a great breakthrough for him," Akash is proud of his friend.

They are still having snacks in the guest room when Aman opens the door.

"Ladies and gentlemen, the paintings are at your disposal. Please come and see and provide your feedback," Aman invites everyone in a jovial tone.

Everyone gets up, leaving the snacks on their plates in the current status.

"Please don't expect anything out of the world," Aman requests everyone as they rush to his room. He doesn't want them to have high expectations from the paintings as he fears that may lead to huge disappointment.

The boys enter the room first followed by Suman and Padma.

Suman whispers to Aman, "Observe Padma as she is looking at the paintings. Don't take your eyes off her."

"Wow! These are awesome!" Akash is already in praise of Aman.

"This is top-class variation," Ghalib responds.

Ayush doesn't respond. He is fighting with his inner self. Even for formality, he is not able to utter a word of praise. Jealousy has the potential to make you do anything.

Aman enters the room after Suman and before Padma. He settles at the corner of the room so he can observe Padma as per his mother's instructions. Padma enters the room and walks a couple of steps. Then, she just stands still, stunned. She obviously didn't expect herself to be featured in the paintings. It seems she has been pranked.

"Wonder!" Suman whispers to Aman.

Aman looks at his mother in wonder.

"Isn't it the expression you are looking for?" Suman says with a smile, pointing at Padma through her eyes.

Aman thanks his mother through his eyes. What can be visible is his salute to his mother.

Aman has captured Padma's expressions in his mind. After everyone leaves, he will create the last painting in the series and name it as Wonder.

"You people cheated me!" Padma shouts with a smile.

"I am sorry. We didn't have any other way out," Suman defends as she holds both her shoulders.

"You don't need to be sorry. I haven't done you any favors. Instead, you have done it for me by getting me painted in such beautiful ways," Padma expresses her gratitude.

They discuss each of the paintings for a couple of hours.

The only question that Padma has is for the painting with the 'love' mood.

The painting features Padma in a bridal avatar, looking at her bridegroom with extreme love.

"This is the only thing that you haven't observed. Is it just your imagination?" Padma checks with Aman.

"Yes! Merely imagination," Aman avoids revealing his dream.

"Why didn't you paint the bridegroom here, mummy? It could be any imaginary character, right?" Akash checks. It's an interesting question and is there in everyone's mind.

"It's about Padma. Her love. It doesn't matter who the bridegroom is," Aman replies instantly. He had expected the question and hence thought of the answer beforehand.

Padma wants to see Aman in the shoes of the bridegroom but can never reveal that to anyone. Such fantasies are meant to be buried in the heart forever.

Everyone starts taking pictures of the paintings on their phones. Tomorrow, the paintings will be gone forever.

"This is my favorite. I will try to recreate it," Akash says while taking the picture of the painting named as 'Love'.

"You needed to paint eight of them, barring the one that was part of the exhibition. Right, mummy?" Ghalib inquires out of curiosity.

Everyone realizes it now. They are all curious to know the answer.

"Right. I will create the last one tonight. You, people, won't be able to see it because they are coming to collect it in the morning tomorrow," he answers.

"Please take a picture of that and send it to us though," Akash expresses interest.

"Sure," Aman agrees to the idea.

"I will stay here. I will have a look at it as soon as it is done," Padma is excited.

The boys leave in some time. One happy, one inspired, and one jealous.

After dinner, Aman starts painting, completes it late at night, and names it Wonder.

Padma, when she looks at it, realizes that the get-together was a scam. It was set up so Aman could see her in the mood of 'Wonder'.

"Does anything in this home happen for real?" she wonders.

:::::::

In the morning, Padma leaves for the store. She is no more in a denial mood. She has accepted that she loves Aman, and she has decided that she will never let him know about it.

Aman sends all the paintings to the art society as their vehicle arrives. He now knows that Padma is the love of his life and makes up his mind to let her know about it at the right time. It's up to Padma to react to it in whatever way she wants. But that shouldn't stop him from expressing himself.

Chapter 11: The Return Call

There are a few consignments that need to go today. Padma is super busy checking, counting, and making sure all is well with the consignments before giving the green light. She spends the whole day performing the required tasks. She has even skipped her lunch. After everything is done, Arvinder approaches Padma.

"Thank you, Padma. You were so good today. You know it is so difficult to manage all this without support. I am so lucky you are managing everything so well," he expresses his happiness.

"Thank you, uncle. I am glad I am able to do what you expect from me," Padma tries to sound humble.

Suddenly, Arvinder realizes something.

"Padma, did you have lunch? I haven't seen you taking a break even for a minute today," he inquires in a concerned tone.

"No, uncle. I am not hungry yet," she says.

"Please don't do that. Always eat on time," Arvinder says. "Bablu," he calls out to an employee.

A boy, around 16 years old, arrives. "Yes, sir," he says in attention position.

"Go to Hotel Ashirvad and get a parcel from there for Padma didi," the boss commands.

"Okay, sir," Bablu says and then realizes something is missing in the statement.

"Sir, what will I get in that parcel?" he checks.

Arvinder gets irritated. "Who is going to have it?" he questions.

"Padma didi," Bablu replies.

"Then, ask her. Why are you asking me?" he says and leaves the spot.

"Didi, Mogambo got angry. What would you like to have?" Bablu checks with Padma.

"Hey, don't call him by that name," she gets angry with the boy.

"Sorry," he says. "Okay, tell me, no, what do you want to have?"

"What will you like to have?" Padma checks with Bablu.

"You tell me. I will have it from the usual roadside hotel," Bablu says.

"No, we will have lunch together today. Say, what will you like to eat?"

Bablu is super excited. Nobody treats him so well. He knows Padma is not joking.

"Didi, can we have biriyani?"

"Why not? Go to that hotel and bring two parcels of biryani. Say Arvinder sir will pay the bill."

"Sure, didi," Bablu says and runs to the hotel. After a long time, he will have biryani today. Last time when Arvinder was happy for some reason, he had ordered biryani for the whole staff.

Bablu comes back in half an hour, and they go to the cabin to relish the food. Padma must have put two spoons of biryani in her mouth when she gets a call. She receives the call subconsciously.

"Hello," she utters.

"Hello! Padma?" Sounds like Venkat's voice.

"Who?" she checks to confirm.

"It's me. Venkat," he says from the other end.

Padma, unable to decide what to do, hangs up. She gets anxious. She sits on the chair nearby and gets lost in her thoughts.

"Didi, won't you eat your biriyani? What happened?" Bablu asks once he finishes off his portion of the food.

"Bablu, I don't feel like eating. Will you be able to eat my portion as well?" Padma checks with him.

"Why not? We shouldn't waste food," Bablu says and starts eating the biriyani from Padma's plate. Who knows when he will get to eat so much biryani or to say the minimum, biryani.

Once Bablu is done with lunch, he cleans the table and the plates and leaves the cabin. Padma keeps sitting there like a lunatic. Her phone keeps ringing.

"Suman!" Padma calls out as she enters the kitchen.

"Oh wow! What a pleasant surprise! Came here directly from the store?" Suman asks in excitement.

"Yes. And I am staying here tonight. Need to talk to you."

Suman is more than happy to have Padma's company today. They will have a good chat the whole night.

The girl stands like a statue in the kitchen as Suman is busy cooking.

"What happened? You are not saying anything? All good?" Suman checks after a few seconds.

The maid, Uma, is around, and Padma doesn't want to reveal everything in her presence.

"I need to talk to you," she says.

"Yes, talk!" says Suman.

Padma doesn't say anything. She waits for Suman to look at her. And when Suman does so, Padma hints to her to go to the guest room.

Suman understands the urgency of the matter. She nods her head and goes to the guest room.

"Venkat called me," Padma whispers as she locks the room from the inside.

"What!" Suman's heart pounds on hearing it. Padma is normal as some time passed since she got the news.

"He called when I was having lunch late in the afternoon," Padma narrates what happened earlier today.

:::::::

Padma didn't pick up Venkat's call for some time. Her phone continued buzzing. After a few attempts from him, she thought of listening to his side of the story.

"Hello!" she said in a rude tone as she received the call.

"Padma, it's me. Venkat," he said.

"I know. Why did you call me now?" she asked in an intimidating tone.

"To say, I am sorry. I had no other choice than to come back home," Venkat tried to defend his case.

"You didn't have any option than to leave a girl you eloped with in the middle of nowhere?! You could have at least informed me! Instead, when I tried calling you, you switched off your phone," Padma shouted at him.

"I know. I was nervous. I didn't dare talk to you. I feared you would not allow me to go back home," he said. "Amma fell sick after we eloped. The doctor said she would die if she didn't come out of the shock that I gave her. She had to see me in front of her," he continued.

"I don't mind you going. Only the informing part went wrong. How could you just leave the girl you eloped with alone? Your mother had so many people around her. I had none. I couldn't even go back home. I could have died. Then, who would you have talked to now? My ghost?" Padma screamed.

Venkat went silent. He didn't have an answer.

"And why are you calling me now?"

"I tried to call you many times before, but you had changed your phone number. Your family had filed a case against me. I was there at the police station for some days. I was out on bail and was instructed by the police not to go out of Srikakulam until the case was closed," Venkat informed.

"Is the case still going on?" she asked.

"No. After you appeared in front of the police, they dismissed the case."

"Can you elaborate on what happened after I appeared in front of the police?" Padma was curious to know.

Venkat described the story as it happened.

The police called both their fathers to the police station and informed them that Padma had come to the police station and given her statement in favor of Venkat. Hence, they needed to shut the case.

Padma's father was shocked to learn about it. He almost got a heart attack when the inspector revealed that the fifth boy in that group was Padma.

Following that incident, Appa Rao who had never befriended an enemy approached Srinivas and apologized. After many attempts from Appa Rao, Srinivas finally agreed to forgive Venkat and his family. Their wives played an important role in convincing the two old men to bury the hatchet.

Padma listened to the entire story from Venkat. She was relieved that back in Srikakulam, the two families did away with their enmity.

"Okay. Good for you then. I have to leave now. I am hanging up," Padma said after listening to the entire story.

"Padma, I wanted to tell you something," said Venkat.

"Okay. Tell me fast. I am in a hurry," she said.

"There is good news. Our parents have agreed to our marriage," Venkat revealed, thinking Padma would be excited to know this.

Padma showed no emotions. She just hung up.

When she wanted to get married to Venkat, their families fought with each other, which forced her to elope. When she was living her life without expecting anything from anyone, they wanted her to get married to the same guy.

In life, it's not always about what you want to happen, it's also about how you want it to happen. In Padma's life, sometimes, the 'what' was missing, and sometimes, the 'how' was missing.

Chapter 12: The Churning

"What would you do, Suman, if you were there in my situation?" Padma asks as they get off the Metro train.

Suman walks quickly. Padma needs to run to catch up with the speed.

The two friends have decided to ditch the men and move around Delhi by public transport. The day is going to be memorable for them for all the kinds of experiences they are getting. The best part of the city is that no matter where you are, there is a train that goes to your destination.

"What can I tell you? If I were in your shoes, maybe I would never go back to a person who has ditched me once," Suman says bluntly.

"But then…?" Padma tries to argue.

"Do you really want to know, Devi, what is right and what is wrong?" Suman asks.

"For what else will I check with you then? Why do you ask me this question?" Padma gets a little irritated.

Suman doesn't care. As a good friend, she needs to provide the right advice, even if it is ruthless.

"Look at the bag you are carrying, Devi. You have a pair of sandals in it, right?" Suman asks.

"Yes, the sandals I bought from the mall," Padma confirms.

"Why did you buy it?"

"Because I always wanted to buy this kind of sandals," Padma answers a bit suspiciously. She is not sure how relevant the question is to the dilemma in her life.

"There were many varieties available in the shop. Many colors and variations to the same pattern. Why did you choose this particular pattern?" Suman further checks as they exit the metro station.

"Because once I saw this pattern in my office. A girl was wearing it. I had it in my mind that I would wear the same pattern one day," Padma answers.

The bus arrives. They enter the bus. Padma follows Suman eagerly. What is she trying to explain? Why is she beating around the bush?

"What is your point?" Padma asks as they take their seats.

"You had gone to the store with a decision. You knew what to buy. Your eyes were glued to those sandals. You were looking for that one thing. Because of that what happened is that you couldn't see all the better options, Devi. By better, I meant, better price, quality, pattern, fitting, anything."

Padma gets into a thinking mode.

"When you go shopping, go with an open mind, Devi. That's all I want to tell you," Suman concludes as she looks at a temple by the road and seeks the blessings of the goddess by offering her prayers silently.

Padma gets what Suman has been trying to say. She has to look at it from a neutral perspective. She cannot let her small-town mentality affect her decisions. To be neutral, she needs to be alone. She cannot even let Suman influence her decisions. She will have to stay away from everyone and take the best call.

When you get a second life, you become more adventurous and open to taking risks. You realize life is worth it. You might not get one more chance. Padma has to make the best call. She has to do justice to the second chance.

"Is it going to make my life any better? Am I having to choose between a rock and a hard place?" Numerous questions run through her mind, and she doesn't have an answer.

"I am again standing at the juncture where I am making a hard decision. I wish the whole time passes in seconds and I meet my fate in the future. I am okay to face it, be it whatever. I just don't like this thinking time, this dilemma," she thinks to herself.

Padma tries to sleep but she hardly gets any sleep. She keeps looking at the ceiling as some visuals from her memories replay in her head. In the morning when she leaves the bed, she feels tired. She doesn't want to go to work today. It won't matter as there isn't much work there. So, she calls Suman and asks her to pass on the message to Mogambo. Yes, she has also started calling him Mogambo after being friends with Suman.

At around 8 am, she freshens up and leaves home to take a stroll. She just wanders aimlessly around the place. There are a lot of people on the road because it's a normal working day and people are going to the office. However, Padma cannot see anyone. It all looks blurry to her. She is lost in her thoughts. She has left the phone in the hostel because she is continuously getting calls from her mother, brother, sister-in-law, and Venkat.

Suddenly, Padma finds a fortune teller under a tree. She doesn't believe in such things but somehow sees value in them today. Hesitantly, she tries to speak to the man with the parrot, "You…"

"Yes, madam. Please sit down," the man reverts even before Padma completes her sentence.

This is good for Padma. She was hesitating to ask the man to predict her future. For the man, it is a normal day. He finds many hesitant customers like her daily. He knows how to make them comfortable and earn money.

"Let's see what the parrot says about your future. Please put 50 rupees on the plate to ask the parrot to come out of the cage and choose the card of your fate," he pitches.

Without thinking much, Padma takes out 50 rupees from her handbag and puts it on the steel plate.

As soon as the money is paid, the man opens the cage. The parrot comes out of it and picks a card from a stack of cards through its beak and hands it over to the boss. The disciplined pet then goes back to the cage where a half-eaten red chili is waiting for it. Nobody knows if the red chili is the motivation or if there are other reasons too, like fear of the boss or following the regular pattern.

"So, madam…" the owner of the parrot starts reading the card. "You had a good past but recently you got into trouble. You are in a dilemma. Going back to your past will help you do away with all your woes. And, let me tell you, if you are not married yet, you are very soon going to get married to an artist," he concludes reading.

Padma wishes she hadn't done this adventurous act. She is more confused now. Venkat is not an artist. She doesn't stand a chance with Aman. She is not interested in any of Aman's artist friends. Her past was good, which means her life with Venkat was good. "Oh my God, this is all rubbish," she says as she swiftly walks away from the fortune teller who is busy placing the 50 rupees currency note safely in his wallet.

After walking for around 10 minutes, Padma ends up in a park. It's filled with lovely pairs across generations. Most of them are taking their morning walk. Some are sitting on benches and chatting. Padma is one of the very few people who are single here. She sits on a bench and keeps watching a toddler playing around their parents. This soothing sight is not enough to calm down the turbulences in the sea of her inner world. She shifts focus and looks at a couple on a bench. The man is resting his head on the woman's lap. The woman has covered the man's face with her *dupatta* to stop the sun rays from falling on his face. Such a beautiful couple! They must have been madly in love with each other. Padma looks at them and revisits her memory lane when Venkat had once rested his head on her lap.

"What will people think? Get up," Padma said.

"They know we love each other, don't they?" Venkat was adamant.

"What if you break up with me? Nobody will marry me if the news of our affair spreads," she complained.

"Why will I do that? Nobody will marry me too," he argued.

"Men are like brass vessels. The more you rub them, the more they shine. That's not the case with women," she counterargued.

"Okay then. You win," Venkat said and attempted to get up.

But he couldn't. Padma was holding him tight so he couldn't move from her lap.

As Padma comes back to the present, she realizes Venkat and she were a beautiful couple as well. One incident cannot be enough to judge a person, can it be? Padma is in the process of forgiving Venkat for his act, it seems. And why shouldn't she forgive him? Barring that one-off incident of going back to Srikakulam without informing her, Venkat had been loving, affectionate, responsible, and supportive all the time.

Looks like, in the game of life with or without Venkat, 'with' is scoring higher.

Padma feels like talking to Aman now. He is a philosopher. He might help her take a decision. She gets up from the bench and leaves the park for Aman's house. She cannot walk now. That will take her time to reach the destination, and she is restless. Therefore, she takes a taxi, which drops her at the destination within no time.

Suman opens the door.

"Come in," she says. "Have you decided what to do?" she checks immediately.

"Not yet," Padma says as she takes a seat in the hall.

Suman goes to the kitchen and comes back with a glass of water. She knows what Padma needs at the moment the most—something that can quench her thirst.

"Drink some water, Devi," she says, offering the glass.

Padma takes the glass from Suman's hands and pours down all the water from the glass into her mouth at once.

"I need to talk to Aman and take his advice, if you don't mind," Padma says quickly while catching her breath.

"Yes. Why will I mind? He has stepped out. Told me he would take a stroll. Will come back in a while. His friends are also coming," Suman says.

Padma gets a little concerned. It will be difficult for her to talk to Aman about her dilemma in front of his friends.

Suman gauges her friend's concerns.

"Don't worry. We will do something about it," Suman says as she places her right hand on Padma's left shoulder.

Padma isn't sure if Suman knows what her concern is. But she is sure Suman will take care of anything.

In some time, the boys arrive. Everyone has arrived with their canvases. Looks like they have planned to paint something.

They all settle in Aman's room.

"Mummy, so what's the theme for today?" Ayush checks as usual with Aman.

"Hmm… let me think," Aman says and starts thinking.

At that exact time, Suman enters the room with a tray of tea.

Ayush shifts his focus to the cups of tea.

"Aunty, can you give us a theme to paint?" He checks with Suman as he picks up a cup.

"I don't know. You people decide for yourself," Suman says and leaves the room.

She goes back to the kitchen where Padma is waiting for her.

"What should I do? Will I get an opportunity to talk to Aman?" Padma asks Suman while biting her nails.

"Looks like they have a full-day plan," Suman says and starts thinking. Suddenly, her eyes glitter as she gets an idea.

"Hey, Devi. Can we discuss your case with everyone without revealing that it's your case? That way, we will have an unbiased outcome," Suman says.

"How is that possible?" Padma looks doubtful.

"Leave it to me. Nobody knows you are in the house. You can eavesdrop and listen to their conversation. What do you say?" Suman asks.

"I don't know," Padma is still doubtful. "And, this is cheating, isn't it?" she asks.

"You and your ethics! Didn't Aman cheat you to create his paintings?" Suman says, ignoring Padma's concerns and walks towards Aman's room.

"Did you guys get a theme?" Suman asks in an intimidating tone.

Everyone gets alert. Something surprising may come from Suman aunty.

"No, aunty. We are still thinking about it. Do you have some ideas? Please feel free to share with us," Akash says as he takes the last sip of tea from his cup.

"Okay. I have an idea. Can you paint a girl in a dilemma?" she proposes.

"Dilemma? For what? Can you elaborate, mummy?" Aman asks.

Suman pretends like she is thinking.

"Suppose Padma gets a call from her parents. They ask her to go back to Srikakulam. Then, she will be in a dilemma, right?" Suman gives the boys a scenario.

"Why will she be in a dilemma? She should go back to her parents if they want to have her back," Aman says without thinking much.

Padma is standing near the door behind Suman, listening to the immediate reactions.

All the boys agree with Aman.

"Yes, mummy is right. Why should there be any confusion?" Someone says and others nod their heads.

Looks like Suman's trick didn't work.

"Okay. Let me modify the scenario a bit more. Suppose her parents call her back so they can get her married to the same guy, what's his name, Venkat. Should she go back and marry him? Won't she be in a dilemma?" Suman says in an irritated tone.

"Aunty, but why do we have to paint her again? Can we get some other theme please?" Ayush pleads.

Ghalib is the only one indifferent now. He is busy scribbling on a paper.

"No, this is a good discussion. Mummy, I think, Padma shouldn't be in a dilemma even then," Aman argues.

Ayush and Akash agree with Aman. Suman looks at Ghalib. Hesitantly, he also nods his head.

"Yes, she shouldn't be in a dilemma. She should go back to her parents and get married to that guy. What's his name? Yes, Venkat," says Akash following which Ayush and Ghalib nod their heads in agreement.

Padma is about to conclude it to be the outcome of the discussion when she hears Aman shouting loudly.

"That guy left her in the middle of nowhere and you people think she should marry him?! This is nonsense," Aman says and throws away the painting brush he was holding.

Suman has never seen Aman in this avatar. He is normally a calm person. Looks like Padma hasn't got the answer yet.

"Aman, so you think Padma shouldn't go back to her home," Suman checks with his son.

Aman tries to sound relaxed.

"Mummy, I think she should go back to her home but definitely should not get married to that guy," Aman says after taking a deep breath.

"Mummy, that guy made just one mistake. Will you judge him for one mistake? What about all the support he gave to her?" Akash argues.

Padma, standing behind Suman, kind of agrees with Akash. If she had a chance to come out in the open and take part in the discussion, she would have given the same argument.

"One mistake! Mistake? It's a blunder, a crime, a sin. And what did it cost? Padma's life, isn't it? Padma would have died. When someone commits such a crime, they don't deserve a second chance. That's my opinion. Rest, you all decide," Aman says and leaves the room.

As Suman moves away from his way, Aman is astounded to find Padma behind her. He would not have been so aggressive if he had been aware of Padma's presence.

Aman looks at both the ladies and steps out of the house.

"Nothing to worry about. He does it whenever he is disturbed. He will come back in some time," Suman tells Padma and moves ahead to take Aman's seat. Padma follows her friend as the latter gestures and sits next to her.

The boys are a little uneasy.

"Padma, you were outside when we were discussing about you?" Ayush asks.

Padma looks at Suman and nods her head.

On seeing this, Ghalib takes a deep breath. "*Good, I didn't comment at all. Saying anything is troublesome in this house*," he thinks to himself.

"Is it a true scenario? Does your family want you to get married to Venkat?" Akash asks.

"Yes," Padma replies.

Everyone goes silent for a minute.

"All of you think I should marry Venkat, right?" Padma checks for confirmation.

"Yes, because…?" Akash becomes cautious in choosing the right words.

"Because…" Suman checks with Akash as everyone looks at him.

Akash thinks for a few seconds.

"I think… because of Tina," he says.

"Tina?"

"Tina?"

"Tina?"

Everyone asks. Some verbally and some non-verbally.

"TINA... T... I... N... A... There Is No Alternative," Akash concludes.

Everyone goes into thinking mode.

Padma decides to accept her fate, go back to Srikakulam, and get married to Venkat. However, she is still in a dilemma slightly because Aman hasn't expressed his decision in favor of her marriage with Venkat.

Suman too is not happy with the decision. But her basis of disagreement is different. She doesn't want her new friend to go away from her. She knows that will be selfish of her. One should do what is right for the moment and good for the future and shouldn't be burdened by emotional baggage when deciding.

Mogambo will not like it when he comes to know about it. Losing an efficient, loyal employee is not good for his business.

When Padma reaches the hostel, she finds around 50 missed calls on her phone. From Venkat, Laxman, Shanti, and Geeta. She calls back to her mother first.

"Hello, amma!"

"Where were you, dear? We called you so many times," Geeta complains.

"I went to my friend's place, amma. Had kept the phone in the hostel," Padma explains.

"How are you? We were worried."

"I am fine, amma."

"Come back home, Padma. Everyone wants to see you here," Geeta gets emotional. It's quite evident from her voice.

"Yes, amma. I am leaving tomorrow," Padma says and asks her mother to take care of herself before hanging up.

Padma starts packing her things for her journey tomorrow. However, she feels a loss of energy. She sits on the bed and cries her heart out. She wishes she could tell someone how she feels now. She wants to call Aman and have a chat with him. Will that make things more complicated? She is not sure.

After struggling for a few minutes with the dilemma, she picks up the phone and gives a call to Aman. No, it doesn't get through. He is busy talking to someone. After a couple of minutes, she dials the number again. Same result.

"How stupid I am! How will Aman have time to discuss my problem? I have troubled him and his family so much. It's high time they should forget me," She thinks as she keeps the phone aside.

The phone rings at the moment. It's Aman's call. Padma takes a deep breath and picks up the call.

"Hello, Padma! Sorry, I disturbed you," Aman says as soon as she picks up the call.

"No, no. I was not doing anything. In fact…"

"I know. You were talking to someone. I called you twice and the call didn't get through," says Aman.

Padma now understands why her call didn't get through.

"How are you? All set to leave for Srikakulam?" Aman asks before Padma says anything.

"Yes, Aman. And I will miss you all," she says.

"Then, don't go," he says.

"You don't want me to go?"

"I was joking. If you are happy that way, you should definitely go."

Padma finally gets the answer. What Akash said about TINA is correct. She will now go back to Srikakulam without any hesitation.

They talk for some time and then hang up.

It's been a week since Padma is back in Srikakulam. She has been showered with love and praise since then. Her sister-in-law Shanti has become her fan. She has been after her to know the entire story of eloping, surviving alone, and coming back. Padma doesn't get tired of telling the story. Who won't like to be treated as a hero? Padma is no exception. After every interval, Shanti and Padma sit together and discuss the story.

Geeta hasn't spent a lot of time with Padma. At first, Padma thought Geeta must have been upset with her, but later she realized that's not the case. Padma is getting married in a week, and Geeta is trying to get used to living without her. However, today she wants to talk to her daughter in private. She has something important to discuss.

Meeting place: Terrace

Time: 5 pm

Excuse: Collecting the pieces of mango and other food items that have been put in the sun for drying

No place is better than the terrace for having a private conversation. It doesn't have walls and hence no ears.

"Tell me, amma, what you wanted to ask," Padma asks as she collects the mango pieces in a basket.

"I am feeling a little uncomfortable asking you about this. I don't know how to start," Geeta says.

"Amma, please don't worry. We are like friends. Go ahead. I don't hide anything from you, do I?" Padma says. "...except for that eloping episode," she adds as her mother looks at her suspiciously.

Geeta thinks for a few seconds. She has to phrase it properly.

"Are you still in love with Venkat? I mean, do you still want to marry him after all that happened?"

"What kind of a question is this, amma? The wedding is taking place next week and you are questioning my willingness!"

"That's not the answer. Tell me if you are 100 percent sure about it," Geeta demands a proper answer.

"It doesn't matter what we want. That's why it's better to keep our feelings inside," Padma tries to avoid the question.

"No harm in telling me, dear. Do you know anyone whom you like more than Venkat? I am not saying I will get you married to him, but telling me will help you feel better," Padma thinks for a few seconds. They have collected all the pieces of green mango. They just settle there to have a chat.

"You know that Aman? He saved my life,"

"Yes, yes, Mr. Kirad's son."

"Yes. I would have loved to have someone like him in my life," Padma says and then realizes she might have gone a little far in the conversation with her mother. "You must be thinking I am talking nonsense," she adds immediately before Geeta reacts.

"No, no, Padma. It's okay. Did you like him?"

"Yes, amma. He is a good guy."

"So, you revealed your feelings to him, and he said he was not interested?" Geeta asks curiously.

"No, amma. How could I tell him? Why will he like me? He won't even pay any attention to girls like me," Padma expresses her fears.

"Oh!" Geeta reacts and takes a deep breath.

"But amma, there were moments I felt he had a liking for me. It might be my misjudgment."

"Moments like?" Geeta gets curious.

"You know he created paintings featuring me in nine moods. One of those moods was 'peace'. So, Suman aunty taught me how to meditate to control anger. She asked me to think of a person or a thing that keeps me at peace. I closed my eyes and started wondering who or what keeps me at peace. My mind directed me to think about Aman. I kept thinking about him for around half an hour. I felt at peace. And, when I opened my eyes, I found him in front of me. He was staring at my face, like a child. For a moment, I thought if it was still a reflection of my thoughts. But no, it was true. He ran away from the room when I found him looking at me," Padma describes the incident as it is.

"Do you think I should have told him?" she checks with her mother.

"Yes. I think so. Because keeping it in your heart doesn't help either. Now, all your life you would think if you had a chance," Geeta reveals her opinion.

"But he is the person who advised I should marry Venkat," Padma says.

"Is it?" Geeta questions.

Padma thinks about it further. "No. Actually, his friends suggested it," she says after recollecting the scene.

"And how did he react when they suggested?"

"He got angry and stepped out of the room," Padma realizes as she answers her mother's question.

"You got your answer. Who knows? You might have missed a chance," they conclude the conversation.

Geeta goes downstairs immediately, but Padma prefers to stay on the terrace for the rest of the evening.

Chapter 13: The Wedding Gift

With Padma gone, the routine in the Kirad family has been affected. Suman cannot call Padma any time because she must be busy preparing for her wedding, which is two weeks from now.

Suman plans to go to Srikakulam to attend the wedding. Even Mogambo will go. But Aman has cited unknown reasons for not going. The four boys have some other plans.

At this moment, Suman is alone at home. The men have stepped out. It seems she has lost her last friend too. She spends the morning and afternoon doing routine tasks. The last few weeks seem like a dream to her. A girl came into their lives and then disappeared.

Before Suman decides to forget Padma completely, her phone buzzes. Yes, Padma has called.

"Hello!"

"Hello, Devi!

"I am sorry I couldn't call you in the last four days. It's really busy here. Nobody is leaving me alone," Padma explains her situation and helps Suman get rid of her doubts.

"No worries. I can understand what you must be going through."

"You are coming to my wedding next week, right?"

"Yes, I am coming."

"And Mogambo?"

"He will also come."

"And Aman?"

"He says he has some important work. I am trying to convince him, but he might not come."

Padma doesn't speak for a few seconds upon hearing this.

"Hello!" Suman tries to confirm if Padma is still there on the call.

"Yes, Suman. I am here. I will be waiting for you. By the way, what are you gifting me on my wedding?"

"I haven't decided that yet, but I think it's going to be the best gift among all you would get."

"I am sure. You will never fail to impress me. It may sound an exaggeration but your presence itself is going to overpower all the gifts I am going to receive," Padma says before hanging up.

The guests from the bridegroom's side are coming home today. They need to discuss the dowry that

the bride's side will give to the groom's family.
Padma has already registered her objection to the
dowry. But nobody is listening to her. Venkat
believes that they should leave it to the elders.
Padma's father wants to give the dowry because it
is a symbol of status in society. The women in the
family have chosen to remain tightlipped on the
matter.

Guests from the groom's side arrive in the
afternoon and they agree that the adjacent land will
be given away in dowry. Appa Rao is going to be
the owner of the entire piece of land after the
wedding.

"It's like you taking your share of the ancestral
property," Geeta explains to Padma when the latter
thinks about it too much.

"Then, it should have been registered in my name.
And, then the choice of taking or not taking it
should be left to me," Padma argues.

The dowry doesn't stop here. The groom's parents
call the shots when it comes to how much cash and
jewelry the bride's parents have to give away apart
from a car.

Padma feels she has become a product of a trade
exchange. She tries to discuss this with Suman who
also advises her to wait and watch and not to
interfere in such matters.

After coming back from Delhi, Padma hasn't got
a chance to meet Venkat either. She doesn't even

know how he looks now. But how much can one change in five months? And how does it matter? Venkat also doesn't know how Padma looks now. It's not about the looks. But the question that bothers Padma is whether Venkat loves her even now. Is it just a trade-off deal? Is it his obligation to marry her because of the whole eloping episode? She doesn't know.

Padma has also revisited her relationship with Venkat many times in her memory lane. She asks herself if she was truly in love with him. Maybe what Akash said is right. At that time too, there was a TINA factor. There Is No Alternative. Venkat was a decent guy in school and college. He studied well. Every girl wanted to talk to him, ask him for notes. Padma craved the proximity of the most popular boy in the vicinity. That's it? Wasn't it anything more? She repents to attempting suicide for such a relationship.

She so wants to discuss all these dilemmas with Suman at the moment, but that's not possible now. Someone or the other is always there around her.

An empty mind is a devil's workshop. Padma knows that. Hence, to do away with the disturbing thoughts, she keeps herself busy with household chores. Her biggest job now is to select sarees, bangles, jewelry, and sweets, and take care of herself so she can look her best as a bride. Every now and then, she applies a layer of turmeric and sandalwood paste on her face.

Aman has become silent lately. He doesn't talk to anyone. He doesn't even hang out with his friends. He doesn't step out. He mostly locks himself in his room. Padma talks to Suman occasionally, and Suman shares the updates with Aman at the dining table, to which he hardly reacts.

"*Something is wrong with this guy*," Suman thinks but doesn't know how to find out.

With Padma gone, Suman spends most of her time with her new friend Lucy. After lunch when Aman steps out for a walk, Lucy enters Aman's room as the door is open. It's time for Lucy to have some milk, hence Suman enters Aman's room in search of the kitten.

Suman hasn't entered Aman's room in the last few days as it has been mostly locked from either inside or outside. She switches on the light. The room looks messy. Paintings are lying here and there.

"*What is this? Aman is not like this. He maintains cleanliness in the room*," Suman talks to herself. She picks up one painting lying on the bed and turns it around. It features Padma. She picks up another. It features Padma. All the paintings lying in the room feature Padma.

"Oh, God! Why couldn't I understand it?" Suman
says to herself and sits down on the bed.
Aman realizes he has kept his room open. He
comes back running to lock it. It's not safe to keep
the door of your heart open. Who can understand
that better than an artist? However, Aman is too
late. He finds Suman in his room, and she looks
really upset.

"I am sorry I came into your room without
checking with you. Lucy came inside. I was looking
for her," Suman says as soon as Aman steps inside.

"That's okay, mummy. I don't think I should lock
the room, or you need my permission to come
inside," says Aman.

"Then, why didn't you tell me about this, Aman?"
Suman asks in a concerned tone.

He doesn't know how to react. He knows that she
knows it now, thanks to the paintings lying all over
the place.

"Because…" he tries to phrase it properly.
"Because there was no use. People would have
laughed at me, and there was no future of it."

"Son, I have told you this in the past and I am
telling you now. You shouldn't accept failure even
before attempting it."

"I am sorry, mummy. I am not a good learner."

"Dear, you don't deserve heartbreak. You are a
good human being. You have people around you to

help you out. You can't keep everything to yourself.
I could have helped you out here."

"You see Padma went to Srikakulam because of
the TINA factor. And now I realize there is no
TINA. You are there."

"But she had already made up her mind to go
back. I didn't want her to feel pressured to return
our favors."

"You are too noble, Aman. I am proud of you. But
these are matters of the heart. And I wanted you to
have a girl like Padma in your life. She is amazing.
When I asked you, you said she was not your type.
So, I never asked you again."

Aman, who is standing like a statue now, doesn't
know what to say.

"By the way, was it love at first sight?" Suman
asks for her knowledge.

"No, mummy. I felt it gradually. Maybe when I
went out with her to find inspiration for my
paintings."

"Oh yeah. I am the culprit then," she realizes.

"Now, don't blame yourself, mummy," Aman
says and hugs his mother. Suman reciprocates the
expression.

The day before the wedding, Suman and Arvinder
reach Srikakulam. The husband didn't want to go to
an ex-employee's wedding one day prior, but the

wife insisted because her relationship status with the bride was different from her husband. Padma is super happy to see Suman around her and be a part of all the wedding rituals.

Suman has got a beautiful gift for Padma. She wants to hand it over to her in privacy. Finally, they are alone in a room where they are choosing the jewelry that Padma is going to wear during the final wedding rituals tomorrow.

"You are very happy, aren't you?" Suman asks.

"Of course! Aman and his friends didn't come. I would have been happier if they were here too," Padma responds.

"Life doesn't give you everything you want. Or let me put it this way. No matter what life gives you, you want more from it," Suman becomes philosophical.

But maybe it's bad timing. Padma is getting married tomorrow. Why will she entertain such thoughts today?

"I am content with my life, Suman. I shouldn't have complaints. Earlier I thought, my life would be better if I didn't have to elope. Now I think, if I hadn't eloped, I wouldn't have met you," she puts it wisely.

"I wanted to tell you something," says Suman at this point.

"Yes, tell me," Padma is ready to pay attention.

"I won't be able to stay here till tomorrow. I will need to leave for Delhi now," says Suman.

"What? You are joking, right?" Padma asks in disbelief.

"No, Devi. I will need to leave. I just came here to give you a precious gift. The best wedding gift one can ever get," Suman says as she hands over a painting to Padma.

"I am leaving now. We are going by train. It will leave the Srikakulam station at 9 pm," Suman adds and hugs Padma before leaving the room. Padma doesn't know how to react. She suspects something fishy here.

It is an abrupt departure. Padma expected Suman to be around during the wedding and reception. She keeps the painting aside and gets busy with the wedding rituals.

It's around 7 pm. The train will leave in two hours. "*Why did Suman leave so early? She has come so far to attend my wedding and didn't wait till the ceremony! She could have spent some more time with me?*" she keeps thinking and gets upset following her best friend's departure. Something didn't go well. Something sounds odd to her.

After an hour following Suman's exit, Geeta enters the room. She wants to say something to her daughter.

"Did you see the painting Suman ma'am gave you?" the mother asks.

"No, amma. The henna on my hands is still wet. I am waiting for it to dry up," Padma answers.

"You can apply henna on your hands again, dear. I hope you don't paint your life wrongly," Geeta says and leaves anxiously.

"Wait! There is something wrong. How does amma know that Suman gifted me a painting?" Padma suspects.

"There must be something fishy. There must be something they know, and I don't. Why will Suman gift me a painting and tell me this is the most precious gift?" Padma keeps murmuring.

She locks the door from the inside and approaches the painting. She unrolls it quickly. And what she finds? It's the same painting that Aman had created for the Hyderabad Art Society. It's portraying the mood of Love. The painting features Padma looking at her groom with immense love. There is nothing new about it. She has seen the painting earlier.

Wait! What just happened now? The henna from Padma's hands got stuck on the painting. Padma looks at her hands. The color from the painting got stuck to her hands as well. Looks like this is a fresh painting, not the one Aman created two weeks ago. While wondering about it, Padma turns it around to check if there is anything on the backside of the painting that she is missing.

Whoa! This is what she missed until now. She doesn't feel the strength in her legs and hence sits down on the sofa lying in the corner. Tears roll down her cheeks. Next to her is lying the painting that features Aman standing with a garland waiting to put it around Padma's neck, who looks at him with immense love.

Padma looks at the clock. It's 8:15 pm. She has to go and meet the Kirads. She opens the door only to find Geeta standing outside. Before she attempts to explain her situation, Geeta hands over a necklace to Padma quickly.

"This is the one that my mother had given me when I got married. I wanted to give it to you. Take it and go marry the person you love and who loves you," Geeta advises.

"He won't ask you for dowry," Geeta adds as Padma takes the necklace from her hands and hugs her before rushing to the Srikakulam station.

Where will Padma find the Kirads? It's a huge station. She is targeting the train at 9. Even if she doesn't find them, she will board that train. It might take her to her destination. However, to her surprise, Padma finds Suman outside the station when she gets down from the autorickshaw.

"Come. Let's go," Suman says.

Padma doesn't know what to say to Suman or how to explain to her why she has come to the station. But it seems like Suman already knows everything. And why won't she know it? Suman is the one who gave Padma the signals through the painting that Aman loves her.

They enter the station and run to the specific platform. The train is about to arrive. Luckily, it is late as usual.

"We need to get a ticket for me," Padma tells Suman as they run.

"Don't worry. We already have it," Suman reveals.

"Are you God or what? You knew I would come?" Padma asks.

"No. I am a mother and a friend. And now I am going to be a mother-in-law too," Suman says as they board the train.

∷∷∷∷

"Let me talk to your mother for a few minutes," Suman requested during one of their conversations a couple of days back.

"Ok, Suman. Here you go," Padma said and handed the phone over to her mother.

"Hello! Who is this?" Geeta was clueless about who she was talking to.

"I am Suman, akka. Padma stayed with us during her Delhi days," Suman introduced herself. By then, Suman had learned they address elder sisters as 'akka' in Srikakulam.

"Wow! Ma'am! I am so glad I am talking to you. Padma told me everything about you," Geeta said as she left everything she was doing and got up.

"Padma is alive because of you people. We are indebted to you. I will never be able to return the favor," Geeta spoke continuously.

"Please don't say that. Padma is like a family member to us, and we don't do favors in the family but perform our duties," Suman responded. "So akka, I wanted to check with you something," Suman added.

"Yes, yes, please tell me." Geeta was ready to pay attention. There was nobody more important than Suman.

"Do you agree Padma got a second life?"

"Yes, madam. I agree. You people have saved her life."

"So, when someone gets a second life, they will want to rectify the mistakes they have done in the past. Do you agree?"

"I agree, madam. But why are you saying this?"

"Suppose Padma loves someone else; will you still get her married to Venkat?"

"No, madam. I will get my daughter married to any guy she loves. This is her second life, and I want her to be happy throughout her life. I won't even mind the caste, religion, or anything of the guy. But we are happy that she loves Venkat and is going to marry him three days from now."

"I hope you are right. I think you are right. But what if there is even an iota of a chance that she is doing it only for her family," Suman talked at a slow pace so Geeta could listen to every word she was speaking.

"We shouldn't let her do so. She doesn't need to do so. We are happy that our daughter is alive and safe. That's all we want now. But what makes you think so, madam?"

"I fear she loves someone else, akka. I am not sure, and I think even she is not sure," Suman revealed.

"What are you saying?" Geeta said and looked at Padma who was checking the fitting of a new dress. She looked happy.

"Can you do something, akka? Padma told me she shares a good bond with you. She told me both of you are more like friends than mother-daughter. Is that correct?"

"Yes, that's correct."

"Then, can you talk to her like a friend and check if she loves someone else?"

"But…"

"I promise I won't bother you regarding this again if she denies it. Can you do this favor for me please?"

Geeta thought for a second and agreed.

After checking with Padma, she called back Suman.

"Madam, you are right. Padma loves Aman but didn't dare express it as she is indebted to you people and doesn't want to spoil the relationship," Geeta informed.

"I feared the same, akka. Even Aman loves Padma but didn't dare express it as he thinks Padma loves Venkat and the revelation will ruin the relationship," Suman said.

"Then, what should we do now, madam?"

"I will visit your home one day before the wedding. We will reveal Aman's feelings for Padma to her and then give her one chance to reconsider her decision. If she agrees, I will bring her with me. If she doesn't, we will accept her decision. Do you agree, akka?" Suman asked.

"Yes, madam. I will do whatever you ask me to do. It's a matter of my daughter's future. I am not ready to compromise with it," Geeta agreed.

"*Mogambo khush hua* (Mogambo is happy now)," Arvinder delivers the line the villain in the movie delivers often as the train leaves the Srikakulam station. He does it loudly in cinematic style. This is embarrassing for the ladies. They didn't know Arvinder was aware of what he was also known as. They start laughing while feeling embarrassed.

Padma whispers in Suman's ears, "Now that I am going to marry your son, what should I address you as? Isn't that complicated?"

"You should call me 'mummy' or 'amma' or 'mom' or 'maa' whatever you want to in public," she replies.

Padma has understood the situation. Life cannot be that easy for anyone. She cannot expect a mother-in-law and a friend in the same person.

"But in private, Devi, call me 'Suman' because that's my name," Suman says and hugs her friend. Padma, relieved of her final woes, holds her friend tight.

❖❖❖

They reach home in Delhi only to find it locked. "Where has Aman gone?" is the question running through everyone's mind. They didn't call him earlier because they thought they would surprise him. But their plan has backfired now.

Suman calls Aman.

"The number you are calling is currently switched off. Please try after some time," the phone answers.

Everyone is worried now. Where has he gone?

Suman calls Akash next.

"Hello!"

"Akash, where is Aman?"

"Aunty, he said he wanted to go to Shimla. He has left an hour back. I wanted to go with him, but he said you people might need me here."

"The car is here. How did he go?" Suman questions, looking at the car in the parking.

"He went by bus."

"Oh! We are back in Delhi."

"He has given me the keys, aunty. I am coming."

Akash reaches in 10 minutes on his bike with Lucy. They enter the house.

As soon as everyone freshens up, Suman says, "We have to go to Shimla. We don't know what Aman is up to."

She spoke everyone's mind. Arvinder has got the keys to the car already. They start their journey immediately.

※:※:※

"Brother, when will the bus that left Delhi at midnight arrive?" Arvinder asks a shopkeeper at the Shimla bus stop as they reach.

"It's already arrived, sir. All the passengers have left. The bus has gone for washing," multiple people at the shop respond.

"Oh, God! Where will we find him now in this big city?" Arvinder wonders.

Everyone tries to call Aman. Same result. His phone is switched off.

Padma is about to break down. She blames herself for this confusion. Suman holds her tight for support. "Don't worry. We will find him. He is not one of those with a weak heart. He won't do anything wrong," Suman gives confidence to Padma.

Suddenly, Akash gets an idea. "Aunty, do you think we should go to the place where we saw Padma first?" he checks.

"Yes, where is that place?" Arvinder asks. He seconds Akash's idea and is in a hurry to execute it.

Everyone gets into the car immediately.

They reach the cliff in a few minutes.

And, what a thrill it is! Everyone is relieved to see Aman sitting on a rock near the cliff. It is the same rock on which Padma sat when the boys saw her the first time.

"Am…" Akash is about to call out Aman when Padma stops him.

She wants to go to the spot from where Aman talked to her for the first time. And, before anyone reacts to her idea, she runs to the spot.

"O, God! Please forgive me. I am coming back to you. I have nobody who loves me. Everyone hates me," Padma speaks loudly. These are the same words she had heard from Aman when he tried to save her.

Aman recognizes the voice and the words.

"What are you doing here?" He comes running to Padma, excitedly.

"What else can I do now? I eloped for the second time. And the boy I have fallen for doesn't know if he loves me. Even I don't know if he loves me."

Aman gauges what is happening now. He looks around to see if anyone else is there. He finds Akash and his parents walking toward him.

As others arrive at the spot, Aman gets emotional and breaks into tears.

"You people helped her elope?" he checks.

"Where there is a will, there is a way, son," Arvinder speaks. It seems he wants to take the entire credit.

"Papa, you did this?" Aman asks in disbelief.

"Yes, but not for you. I needed my assistant back," he answers.

"Now, will you propose to me or I will jump off the cliff?" Padma says while wiping her tears.

"Go, son! Do it," Suman encourages her son.

Aman doesn't want to lose the opportunity. He goes on his knees, holds Padma's hand, and says, "Yes, I love you, Padma. Would you mind being my model for the rest of my life?"

"Yes! Yes! Yes!" Padma says and hugs him. They both continue crying.

As they walk a few steps back from the cliff, they see Ayush and Ghalib painting in a plain area. It's the same spot they were painting at the last time.

"Aunty! Look at this. Isn't this a masterpiece?"
Ayush asks as soon as he finds Suman.

Suman looks at his painting. He has drawn an
outline of Aman sitting on the rock near the cliff.

Suman slaps him lightly. "How long will you be
watching things happen? When will you start being
a part of the happening?" Suman shouts at him.

As Ayush is still thinking about what went wrong,
everyone starts laughing. Arvinder holds Ayush's
hand and starts explaining to him.

All four artists have gathered today to discuss the
wedding of Aman and Padma. Padma has bid
goodbye to the hostel. She is living here which she
calls her permanent home.

"So, out of all of Aman's paintings, which one do
you like the most?" Akash checks with Padma.

"I haven't yet seen all his paintings. I have only
seen the ones I featured in."

"And amongst those, which one is your favorite?"
Akash is curious to know.

"The one where I am in the bridal avatar."

"Oh, that one where you are getting married to
someone?" Ayush speaks loudly.

"Not to someone. The recent one where I am
getting married to Aman," Padma reveals.

"The recent one! Which one?" Ayush wonders
and looks at Aman.

"Mummy, you created another version of the same?" Ghalib inquires.

Akash doesn't know how to react.

Aman is shocked to learn this. "Which one? I didn't create any new version," he reveals.

Suman arrives with a tea tray. Akash looks at her helplessly.

"What happened? You people look so curious," Suman checks.

Padma leaves the room and goes to her room and brings the painting.

By now, Suman has decided to reveal the truth. "Akash painted this," Suman reveals as soon as Padma displays the painting to everyone.

Aman is shocked. Padma is shocked.

"How many favors will you do for me?" Padma asks Suman.

"We are family, dear. In my family, we don't do favors for each other. We perform our duties," Suman says and embraces her daughter-in-law.

The mother and son smile at each other as their eyes meet. "You are the best mother in the world," Aman says through his eyes as Akash presses his hand for emotional support.

"Can anyone please tell me what happened?" Ayush asks curiously to which everyone starts laughing.

Thank you for reading the book.
Other works of the author include:

Novels
The Wedding Picture:
"Do I have another chance?"

14 Nights & The Wedding Gift

For any feedback, please feel free to write to
maharana.ganesh@gmail.com

Printed in Great Britain
by Amazon

27213047R00116